MOOD
SWINGS

Mood Swings

by

Dave Jeffery

BLACK SHUCK
SHADOWS

Black Shuck Books
www.BlackShuckBooks.co.uk

Versions of the following stories first appeared as follows:
'Restoring Scarlet' in *Chromatics* (Lycropolis Press, 2010)
'Last Rose of Summer' in *Spectrum* (Dark Continents Publishing, 2011)
'Masquerade' in *Watch* (Imprint Phoenix Press, 2011)
'Where There's a Will...' in *The Demonologica Biblica* (Western Legends Publishing, 2013)
'Disturbia' (as 'The Great Fear') in *Twelve Dark Days* (Nocturnicon Books, 2017)

Cover design & internal layout © WHITEspace 2024
www.white-space.uk

First published in the UK by Black Shuck Books, 2024

978-1-917173-98-8

Restoring Scarlet

There is beauty in death. I knew this to be true even before I met Scarlet.

And when she came to me on that night in December, she was so very *dead*, so very *broken*, it would have been hard for anyone to see what she had once been.

The car crash had been her catalyst for change; the vehicle had rolled, crumpled, metal and plastic fashioning flesh and bone the way a sculptor's fingers caress clay until it becomes an act of expression; a metamorphosis born of inertia.

Nature has a way of reminding us that we are nothing but fragile creatures. And when it does decide to teach us the realities of life, it is usually in spectacularly undeniable ways.

The coroner's crew brought Scarlet into the parlour. There were two of them. There were always two of them, and it was always Harry Cullen and Phillip Noakes.

Harry was a gaunt, balding man with a pencil thin moustache and lips almost in competition. When he smiled it was an act; his eyes – ice blue and watery – seemed to go through the motions like some third rate animatronic at a fairground attraction. Phillip was a solid youth who had built his body on protein shakes and pumping iron. His uniform – black and made of a material that creaked as he moved – was a snug fit, and his high visibility jacket was barely able to accommodate his sculpted chest.

"Here she is, Doc," Harry said.

The room in which I applied my craft was a large and rectangular space. The walls and ceilings were veneered in white tiles and grouting; a cartoonish, clinical landscape that kicked around Harry's words for a while before allowing them liberty.

"How many times do I have to say I'm *not* a doctor?" I said amiably. It was patter; a game people played to offset the fact our time was entwined with those no longer living. "My clients are dead. On this basis I'd be a pretty poor physician."

Harry chuckled. "Look on the bright side, you never get no complaints."

"This is true."

The silence stalled on the air; hanging out for a moment with the sweet smell of disinfectant. Harry spoke again; his words were quick, as though eager to inject life back into the room.

"Anyway, it's fair to say she's been messed up pretty badly."

Scarlet was inside a misshapen body bag which in turn lay on a highly polished gurney. I cocked my head and raised my eyebrows.

"Been *peeking* again, Harry?"

The comment turned his cheeks to Valentine roses.

"Not in any kinda disrespectful way, Doc."

"Nevertheless, not your place to go looking," I said. I meant it. This was *my* privilege.

"Where's the harm?" Phil grumbled. "Not like she's gonna get pissed at us."

"*Respect* is all we can give her, Phillip," I said. "She is at our mercy, naked and dependent on only the morality we can bring to her final event. Take that away and there really is nothing."

Phil sniffed a response. His face told me he didn't care; his youth detaching him from the concept of ethics and the Long Sleep. In some ways I envied him. Stupidity is often the armour in the war against moral dilemma.

"Anyway," Harry interjected as he removed a bulky, black box from the pocket of his luminous jacket. "Just need you to sign off on her and we'll leave you two together."

He pulled a slim, plastic stylus from behind her right ear and used it to tap the electronic signature device with a series of staccato clicks. After a few seconds he held the stylus out to me, and I scrawled my cyber-signature on the screen as Harry supported the box. His fingers were twig-thin and pale against the scratched plastic.

"There you go," I said handing the stylus back. "Your job ends as mine begins."

Harry gave a mock salute and pointed to the trolley. "The way I feel, it might not be too long before you're seeing me on this gurney." He smiled slightly.

I knew this was no lie. I had heard the tumour in his gut feeding for most of the past few moments. Yes, it was fledgling, a mere dot on his pancreas, but it needed to grow up fast, in ways kids like Phil could never understand. And soon it would be *guzzling* him, turning tissue to blackened soup, growing fat on its purulent juices. It made me a little sad. Despite his untrustworthy eyes, he had a kind heart. Yes, it was a heart that would be stopping for good by Spring, but it would at least allow him to see one more Christmas with his grandkids. Small wins are as great as huge victories in the fight against cancer. It was an honour to be part of his final journey on this earth.

My unique worldview had its moments.

There were no clichés here. My abilities were neither gift nor curse. They just *were*. A simple capacity for being able to tune in to those things that no one else knew existed. I didn't question it. Not anymore, at least.

With a grunt and a sigh, Harry and Phil lifted the body bag carefully onto the slab of surgical steel that was my place of work. They placed Scarlet gently on the shimmering surface and paused to look down upon her, both silent.

"Let's get out of here, Phil," Harry said finally. "I need hot, strong coffee to get the chill of this place out of my bones."

The gurney clattered across the tiles as the two men left me with my charge. I watched them go, my eyes not leaving Harry for a second; knowing that there would come a day when we would meet for one last time as I signed a virtual docket with his name on it.

~

My *ability* had been given a name in the Summer of '77. The christening had taken place in the 10th floor apartment belonging to my Aunt Lucy. We sat on a large sofa, my backside hot from the polyester, my brow coming out in sympathy as I recalled the events that had brought me to her that day. I was thirteen years old and the voices – the *visions* – had begun to surface.

Aunt Lucy was an open woman but closed off from the rest of the family. This was on account of her 'wanton way', as my mother called it. In reality, she was non-conformist, non-traditional, the proverbial polar opposite to her sister – my mother – who had been married for an aeon, a full time home and family maker. My mother held such values in esteem and fiercely rejected anything that contested her blueprint for the perfect life.

"Mum said I should stop eating so late at night," I said. "That's what gives me the dreams."

"Well, your mum was always the practical one." Aunt Lucy smiled. "If detergent doesn't work, then she'll fall back on old wives' tales."

"So she's wrong?"

"What do *you* think?" Her response was quick-fire, catching me off-guard. She scrutinised my eyes as she played with a button on her black cardigan.

Unlike her response, I pondered for a while.

"They don't seem like dreams," I offered in the end.

"Then they are clearly *not*," she sniffed as she reached for her mug of coffee.

"But they *are* scary," I said. "Just like bad dreams."

"What you see – what you hear – are only scary because you don't understand them," she said. "You call them dreams because you try to explain it to yourself. And your mother will always encourage the safer option."

"What if I don't *want* to understand?" I'd made the comment with a sulky air.

"Whether you do or don't, this thing will still be part of you," she said firmly, over the brim of her coffee mug.

The air was heavy, and I felt as though the weight of it was crushing me. My aunt seemed to sense my despair. When she spoke again, her tone had been soft, and careful.

"You remember when you first had that bear of yours?" she asked.

I looked at her puzzled, the question not registering straight away. Then I understood. She was referring to Goliath, a battered brown teddy bear I had carried around with me for most of my early years. Goliath was now sitting on a shelf in my bedroom, not often thought about nor handled. But he was always there looking down on me.

"Goliath?"

"Goliath, of course," she said with a whimsical smile. "That's the fella."

She placed the mug back onto the table and knitted the fingers of both hands together in her lap. "I remember when your dad brought that moth-eaten thing into the house. He said he'd won it at some card game. More likely he found it in a skip. Thing is, you fell in love with that lump of fur from the moment you set eyes on it. But, if you remember, even though you took it everywhere in that first week, you told your dad you still didn't feel as though it belonged to you on account of you not being the first one to own it."

I must have looked totally bemused because she'd laughed and leaned forward as though this would help me to understand better.

"What I'm saying is, you never truly felt that bear was yours until you gave it a *name*. It's the same with your ability. You need to name it, so it becomes yours. Maybe – just maybe – you'll grow to accept it."

"I suppose it does make sense," I said doubtfully. "Shall I give it a proper name? You know, like a *name*, name?"

"You can do whatever you want to do. Call it whatever you like. It just has to mean something to you."

"Maybe I can call it *Faith?*"

This time it was Aunt Lucy who was left surprised by my reply.

"Having belief is a gift in itself," she said casually. "It is a wise choice."

"I chose it because it's *your* real name," I explained.

"So it is," she said, and I knew she was pretending not to have realised, but I went along with it. "I never use it, so you are certainly welcome to it."

"Don't you like it?"

"I never had me much faith in things as I grew up," she said with a wink.

"Don't you have faith in *anything?*"

"I have faith in you, my dear boy," she grinned. "That's enough at my age."

~

As I got older, I discovered that Faith could, indeed, mend that which was broken. But there were rules; perverse rules that were as equally confounding as the existence of Faith itself. I first discovered this when I was working a summer job at a landfill site while I waited for the university to reopen for the autumn semester. I was 20 years of age and Faith was no longer a brash entity, it had become subtle, controllable

– a thing that could be detuned to static noise. Yes, at night, in the cerebral space between consciousness and sleep, some folks did get a little *insistent*, but overall, it was nothing a bottle of Merlot couldn't fix.

Then came the incident with the dog.

It was in one of the skips designated for garden waste. One of the full-time site managers, an Irish Neanderthal who went by the name of Brendon Hartley, volunteered my services to retrieve it. He didn't hide his glee at having a 'freeloading feckin' student' climb into a huge metal crate, rammed with chopped grass, twisted offshoots of rose bushes and lacerating brambles that a hundred and one harassed weekend horticulturalists had mercilessly hacked from their gardens.

But amongst all the redundant foliage was the apparent corpse of a Yorkshire terrier. One of the punters had seen it and informed Hartley, who had put his thick fists on his fat waist and hollered my name.

I had climbed the access steps – ten metal strips leading to a small, enclosed platform which overlooked the skip – and reluctantly peered over the edge. I could see the dog pretty much straight away. It lay semi-covered in bracken, its sandy coloured muzzle apparently frozen in a snarl; tongue a limp, pink pennant curling under its lower jaw.

The skip was three-quarters full. A few more deposits and the JCB would've been ordered to compress the contents with its bucket to allow for a few more litres of space. Instead, I had to clamber over the side of the skip and drop down five feet or so, landing unceremoniously on my arse amid a coarse mound of branches. I stood, cursing as I was momentarily destabilised by the haphazard surface underfoot. Precariously I made my way across the undulating landscape until I stood over the animal. Up close I noticed something even more unsettling.

The dog wasn't dead.

Sure, it wasn't long for the world, but there was dull life in its eyes. It had a red nylon collar emblazoned with the name *Buster* in white letters.

I squatted and reached for it, my intention to grab hold of the collar and drag Buster away from its coat of foliage. I hooked my index finger beneath the collar and then it happened.

Initially the sensation was akin to a burst of static, the kind where fingertips connect with an old TV screen. There were small tendrils of electricity; I remember them vividly as they danced in the space between the dog and my fingers. However, there was no pain, just a tickling under the cuticles.

There was a sound; small pops and cracks as, to my horror, Buster's small body began to undulate as though a thousand unseen creatures were writhing beneath his skin. Under my gaze his whole body inflated and suddenly a small pathetic hiss emerged from the muzzle, as the dog's bewildered eyes rolled to their whites. The hiss became a growl, low at first, but rising to a snarl as the animal fought against the unbearable pain I had somehow triggered. My response was instant, driven by pity, fuelled by instinct; I reached for Buster's head, took it in my hands (almost letting go as I felt the bones of his skull rippling against my palms) and staying determined enough, feeling responsible enough, to fulfil my duty, I snapped Buster's neck with one anti-clockwise turn. The sound was like dry leaves crunching underfoot during a woodland stroll.

I'd looked up to see if anyone had seen my actions. But no faces peered down into the skip, Hartley having clearly grown bored and gone on to other jobs. The guilt grabbed my innards and tugged at them a little before realisation that I had somehow caused this thing – whatever this *thing* was – to happen.

So much suffering at my hands. It was difficult at that point not to challenge my aunt's views that Faith was not a terrible curse that could only bring bad things to the world.

Ten years later, on the day of Aunt Lucy's funeral, I decided to rethink this as a concept.

~

Aunt Lucy died of 'natural causes' at the age of 91. Her aged heart had just given out, the spark that had powered it extinguished for good.

By all accounts she had been dead by the time she hit the street; a small mercy given that the delivery truck she'd fallen under was doing about forty miles per hour and dragged her over 100 yards before its brakes kicked in with such a squeal, they had almost drowned out the screams of onlookers.

I wasn't aware of any of this until the day of the funeral. Mum and Dad had kept information under wraps almost as effectively as Aunt Lucy's mangled body. There was a clue in that there was no open coffin. I pressed my parents for a reason until, with some irritation, my mother said they didn't feel it was appropriate given my aunt's 'accident' and it was 'better to remember her as she was'. I quietly refuted this and decided to go and pay my own respects to Aunt Lucy, away from prying eyes. Given that my parents spent most of their life looking in the opposite direction to me, it was easy to slip away unnoticed and go and seek out my aunt's casket.

Faith had paid a visit as I sneaked into the parlour, a place with half-height wood panelling and bland, cream walls. The room commanded a solemn air, where dust motes were tinted blue by the shafts of light coming through the high arched window, and the air was perfumed with the sickly stink of lilies and roses. Just as my parent kept the nature of Aunt Lucy's demise from me, so had they kept it from the world; a closed casket hiding the sins of her passing. I can't explain it, the need to see my aunt. Outsiders and psychologists may have considered such a desire the trappings of a macabre and maladaptive mind. I saw it simply as a final farewell.

The yearning to see my aunt became more insistent as I neared the coffin. It was a magnificent mahogany piece, and I watched my reflection grow on its highly polished surface; a distorted elongated shadow that made about as much sense as my actions that day. The lid was in two sections, and with a faltering heart, I took a deep breath and lifted the smallest of these and peered inside.

Aunt Lucy no longer had a face. Yes, she had a nose and some teeth, but the shape of her head was that of a concave spoon, all her features staved in to the point where I wasn't sure for a few seconds what I was actually looking at. The shroud was a billowing rag that was three sizes too big, but I knew in that instant its shapelessness was to cover the terrible damage inflicted on her frail body. I took an involuntary step backwards; questions pummelling my brain, aiding the momentum.

How had this happened? Why did she look like this? Couldn't they have done something to make her better? Make her *presentable*?

It was then that Faith decided to drop a few things into my head. The first was an image of Buster in the skip. Just as instinct had initially driven me away from the casket, so this image pushed me forwards and my trembling fingers moved through space towards Aunt Lucy's brutalised face.

Something was screaming inside my head, my rational thinking suddenly free of grief and loss. And in its screams, it tried to remind me what had happened to the dog, the torment that I momentarily brought to its final moments. But this was a world with Faith, and in such a world reason had no place.

My fingertips connected with traumatised skin made pale from thick greasepaint, and at once I was overcome with a sensation akin to tranquillity. My heart stalled and my mind emptied of the psychological tempest that had been battering it only seconds before. It was not merely the eye of the hurricane; it was as though I were not only experiencing the ethereal plane, I was now part of its landscape. And I sensed that, because my mind was now empty, it had become a vessel into which those things we consider without reason could come forth, pouring into a consciousness now welcoming and receptive. And what did come forth was the story of a life – Aunt Lucy's life, I saw it flicker-flash through my mind, my synapses now a server streaming online movies, telling her story: images of a baby in the arms of its nursing mother, blouse lifted up so it could suckle on breasts engorged with milk; a toddler exploring small, bare rooms, steered away from an open fire dancing in a stone hearth as tendrils of smoke drifted into the sparse living room; a whiteout replaced by a classroom, rows of small wooden desks in front of a huge blackboard, a stern male teacher pacing the room, looking down at his small pupils in flimsy grey tabards shivering in cold and fear; another whiteout and then Aunt Lucy as a young woman cuddling up to a handsome young man in a theatre as they watch a black and white film, the man more interested in putting his hand inside her blouse, she giggling and slapping it away; more whiteouts, rapid, punctuating a life as it streamed through my consciousness until the final moments when, in a city street the images suddenly winked out. But it was only for a moment before more images poured in: the vast shape of a truck, its oncoming wheels huge, then the haphazard images of a chassis and kerbs and buildings and the horrified faces of people, mouths: black holes as they watched her demise. These were not her memories – her experiences – somehow, I knew it. They were the images of whatever powers determine the existence of Faith. I felt no horror in it, just an overwhelming sense of privilege. And when I heard Aunt Lucy's small insistent whispers, the sense of peace was reinforced in ways I had never known before, and I suddenly looked upon her in the casket and she was no longer a broken shell, she was lying there, at peace, her face restored and beautiful in its serenity, and my tears flowed with the same ferocity as the pictures had in my mind.

I had closed the casket lid, ashamed that I had to leave the profundity of the moment in darkness, but her incoherent, soothing mummers were not left behind. Instead, they came with me and for many years were the tune to which I constructed a life.

~

The day at the funeral home was to be my epiphany. I had the ability to mend that which was broken. There was no denying it. No, I was no Saviour destined to make the dead walk again, but I could restore them to what they were in life. And in this I found duty. I found *purpose*.

I jumped through the hoops, perpetuated the facade: attended school, became qualified in the science of embalming; acquired licenses, a small business and then, as news of my work spread to the mourning populous, I gained my reputation. I'm considered a genius in my field; someone who is unique. I can only lay claim to one of these adjectives. I am unique in that my Faith is very different to that of the average person. My Faith restores in a very real sense. I have no need for the large copper embalming tank that stands inert and glittering to the left of the preparation table. I have no use for the line of gleaming surgical tools sitting on the shelf. These are mere props in my perpetual theatre of deception.

So now I stand over Scarlet and look down upon her shattered remains. Her right arm is a zigzag born of multiple fractures, her belly is a balloon distended by gas and trauma and the puckered, Y-shaped post-mortem scar is struggling to cope, the stitches and skin arching in places like struggling buttons of a glutton's shirt. Her legs are still intact, muscles mottled by bruising, but her left leg is dislocated to the extent where her foot is backwards. Her face is a bloated mass of trauma tissue. Both her eyes are crudely sewn shut and most of her teeth, framed by inflated purple lips, are gone. One incisor stands tall, but its triumph is as token as it is pointless.

"Oh, my," I sadly mutter. "What has this world done to you?"

I will know soon enough. It is part of the process – part of the ritual – that will unite us forever. I will restore Scarlet and she will tell me her secrets. It is how this works; how this has always worked since that first day with Aunt Lucy.

I stroke her hair with my palm and in this small act Scarlet's world is made plain to me; every moment of her all-too-brief existence on this Earth. Good times, bad times; I see her laugh, I watch her weep, I see the days that she will forever hold dear and those she would choose to forget; I watch her climax for the first time; I watch her die in a violent explosion of glass and metal. I am an ethereal voyeur to passing moments and as her life becomes unbridled and laid bare before me, so her shape begins to morph into what she once was.

Change is not genial. It comes with the sharp snaps and pops as bones repatriate. There are other noises: sucking and slopping sounds as organs shift in her abdomen; the wet-leather creak of sinews and muscles as they tighten. I hear all of this, but I see only Scarlet, her memories, her *life*. And by the time I look down upon her perfectly reformed countenance, gaze into eyes that are as blue ice, I have begun to weep. It is not sorrow I feel at this moment, it is a fathomless reverence that holds me beguiled and time is suddenly meaningless; only she is important.

This is how I stay for several minutes and then I come back to the room, to the job that needs to be done before Scarlet can join the *others*.

~

There came a point where those I *mended* became a part of me. I can't put my finger on it, but I shared so much of their experience; the process of *re-mending* making us symbiotic. For a while I tried to ignore it, but as time moved on the sense of guilt as I gave them back to their loved one – beautiful and unbroken – tore my heart asunder; a physical agony that left me in mourning for weeks afterwards every time I said goodbye.

Perhaps it was this that changed the way I now do things. Perhaps it was the inevitability of being so in touch with my Faith. Like the body, the mind is an equally fragile thing. Did it give in, buckling under the psychic pressures of accepting Faith? I no longer question it; I merely accept that this is the way it must be in order for no one to mourn forever. It is reciprocal; it is how I redress the balance.

Once I let them in, I cannot let them go. It is a failing on my part perhaps, a weakness. But such is the nature of emotional investment. Those who are touched by Faith are drawn to me, and I to them. Their relatives want to see their dearest departed fixed and cosseted in the casket. I am the architect of this wish, and I am not one to deny such an injunction. Soon latex moulds will create a Scarlet mask, the mannequin will wear one of her favourite dresses, Scarlet will be as they remember her. It will not actually *be* her, but an effigy that will receive their mourning tears. It is a quiet deception, but one in which everyone is satisfied; everyone is able to love and give their farewells.

All except me, of course. I can never say goodbye. That is why the real Scarlet will stay with me. That is why they *all* stay with me.

~

There, I have finished. Scarlet's waxen, latex doppelganger lies in its casket ready to receive her kin. She looks peaceful but, above all, she looks *real*. For those who place their lips on her brow in a parting kiss she will *feel* real. I am a master at my craft.

Some may call me a thief. Others, those of a more vulgar constitution, may even sneer 'body snatcher'. And why not? They are terms I have served upon myself at one time or another. But I am able to rationalise who I am, *what* I am. I have restored those who have endured destruction. I leave their loved ones with memories from which they can draw comfort. I give more than I take. Faith is the vehicle that allows substance to the incorporeal and I am their safe keeper. And keep them safe I do, in a place where they are worshipped like deities in their clandestine church beyond the door.

So it is with irredeemable virtue that I scoop Scarlet from the table, coveting her in my arms as I take her to the door at the far side of the room. Her cheek rests on my shoulder, and inside my mind her soft murmuring puts me at ease, cosseting any remorse at my pending actions.

The door is non-descript, yet it is a gateway to reverence. As always, as I cross the threshold, a tear falls from my chin and into Scarlet's soft, dark hair. It nestles in the ebony strands as a small clear blister before it is absorbed, becoming part of her.

There is a corridor beyond the door, it is short and has grey walls and is lit by low wattage bulbs that hang from electrical cable in the ceiling. It would not meet standards but as far as anyone else is concerned, this place does not exist.

As I move down the corridor, I make sure that Scarlet is held close to me; I snuggle up to her in a show of comfort. Her murmurs tell me she never wants me to let her go. I assure her that we want the same thing: to be together for whatever eternity holds for us. We reach a flight of concrete steps that lead down into the darkness.

We descend and our footsteps echo, betraying that we are moving into a larger space; a place that does not feature on the building schematics. There is cool air about us, and the machine-hum of an air conditioning unit orchestrates our movement. Motion sensors in the ceiling blink twice, triggering the lighting below.

The cave is the size of a basketball court. There is tiered seating at the far end, hewn into the stone, and rising high. The front row is a mere twenty feet away as we move away from the staircase. We pass a podium that sits centre stage. I carry Scarlet beyond the podium to the edge of the rostrum, where we descend another short run of steps, past several cots and baby car seats lined in a neat row. I delicately place her in a vacant stone seat, adjusting her dress, making her *decent*. Before leaving her, I place a delicate kiss on her brow and I hear her sigh. It brings me warmth against the frigid air.

I climb the steps and make my way to the podium, looking out at the audience, looking *upon* them. As always, it is as though I see them for the first time. The love for them grabs my heart, making it almost impossible to breathe. I see young faces, old faces; those in between. Men, women, and children; mothers and fathers; sons and daughters. They are all perfect, all *mended*; their eyes are open and locked onto mine. They all whisper to me, and I am able to hear every single one of them.

I have doubts, but never when I am here, with *them*. These are my family beneath the earth: reverent, tranquil. Comforted.

Each of us unequivocally united by Faith.

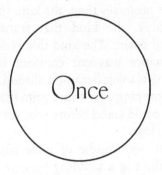

Once

You are there again, standing by the window, gazing out upon the garden, seeing something I cannot, like a secret, carefully and expertly kept. As clockwork, this routine; a late-night affair where confusion seems to be the only available suitor. Or the only one with whom you feel at home.

The cottage is cool, the bedsheets a warm memory; the hearth of the fireplace is as dark as these current times, ever waiting for some spark to tend the kindling and bring back the faded light of hope to my weathered heart. Watching you – the sentinel frozen in a private vigil – puts distance in this cramped space; we are empty as the void, and as vast as the cosmos.

Things were so different, once. Do you remember those days in Worcester, the river walks where the air was heady with the scent of summer; the surge and rush of the river Severn as it traversed the weir? Holding hands, stolen kisses under gloomy bridges, smiles bright, eyes only for each other in those lazy yet lengthy moments. We made promises then, the kind that cement relationships, the kind that transcend love and carnal desire. The kind that well and truly last. Romance was our comfort, but all too quickly the blanket became a shroud, the world opaque, trapping us within a grim reality, where someone could stand before you, yet you would remain so lost.

A scuff and shuffle of mule slippers over the pile, the rug a wedding present from your mother. Now it is aged and she, quite dead. I watched you mourn her, my arm wrapped about yours, the sky a dull iron, our hearts just as heavy. Was this where it all began, I wonder, this infernal distance? Is this what keeps you here on this earth, near yet so far away from my love, from what it used to mean, and the way it used to solve so many of your ills? Like you with your mother on that grey and sullen day, I also grieve, but for you, for the person you were before these moments of private counsel where I am nothing more than a mere observer.

I am bitter, sour to the point of curdled cream. Sometimes it eats through what little solace I find, until the forlorn stink of dread and hopelessness threatens to suffocate. In the clutch of ragged breath, I have watched our tiny world turn, while I grip the breakfast bar or dressing table so I may remain steadfast and upright. So I may present this resolute persona. Spinning rooms stir up memories.

Things were so different, once. Do you remember our date at the ice rink in Tamworth? You said I looked like Bambi on ice, and I said you talked in clichés. You laughed, that infectious guffaw, and said "touché!" Later that day, we had dinner at Portobello, and you told me you loved me more than tortellini before putting on your meaningful face and saying with all earnestness that I was your world, and you'd never leave. Neither of us knew how hollow such a promise was to become; a sentiment and a curse fused as love.

Love. In this netherworld you now inhabit, is love the same? Can it *be* the same? Do you look at me with those empty eyes and feel anything at all? It seems that you are searching for something. Perhaps it is a place I cannot possibly know, or there is something beckoning, the way a party magician beguiles a child with cards and glitter. I cannot possibly know, of course. I am as much in the dark as the kindling in the grate. Yes, you are here, and yet you are not, standing on a threshold between worlds: yours, and mine.

Things were so different, once. Do you remember little Dotty? She was meant to be a celebration, a testament to our life together. But no life in the end; in the stifling heat of a maternity suite she was unmoved, tiny, and still, slick with blood and meconium; a frantic suction machine orchestrated her passing. In her loss we found strength, the means to heal. We found such a thing in each other, building walls of a castle keep that kept everyone else at bay. In that time, we shared the pain of loss, and deemed it an experience not worthy of repeating. A way to accept what the doctors had already told us in that small stuffy room, where the only response was the hum of a desk fan and our weeping, put on mute.

Fingers on the glass, a tiny tattoo: the rhythm of the lost. The pane is clear, unlike my thoughts as I move towards you like you're some kind of explosive device set to detonate at the slightest vibration.

Things were so different, once. Do you remember when we could not wait to spend hours in each other's bed? Talking and exploring, getting to know each other's mind and body, savouring every second, like we somehow knew time would one day betray us. Sometimes back then, we kept our peace; words devolved to deeds and touch. Now, when we need them the most, words fail us. They make their escape and roam free, yet they never quite connect, not the way they used to, not the way they *should*. They are the petrified prehistoric remains; they are the silent screams of those drowning in their own shallow lives.

So, too, was the onset of our woe subtle and insidious. That time I found you putting the tea caddy in the fridge, and for a moment you thought that's where it truly lived. Then that 'tut, tut, tut' as reality dawned, part mirth but darkened by quick irritation, and fear.

Things were so different, once. Do you remember the days after the nights before, thick heads and bacon rolls, resuscitation by caffeine and ketchup? You were telling me things more than once, even back then; so in this maybe things are the same. But it is the only thing, and I have no one to blame but the cruelties of life. Maybe, if had a little faith in a god or the medics, it might distract me from this, the day-to-day, and these cool nights when I am pulled from sleep as you tap that damned window. Is there any point to it, any point *in* this, the same day playing on repeat? If only I could break into that brave new world you are desperate to find. Perhaps that tapping on the pane is a staccato message to the beyond, and one night when I shuffle from our bed and come to this window, you will be gone and only that tapping will remain. The thought brings a shudder, the cold touch of fear does its work, and I pause, no longer keen to place a gentle hand upon your forearm and guide you back to bed.

I spurn my reticence; ashamed that for a moment I am afraid of you, of what you have become, a mere shadow of the person you were, a ghost lost and alone. Is this not an example of why I must persevere, muster the resolve – mental and physical – to ensure you know that I am with you, always?

Things were so different, once. Do you remember those first crisp winters in our small apartment in Bromsgrove, drinking hot chocolate from big red mugs, marshmallows bobbing against our lips; blankets about our shoulders, the cold turning our breath to steam? We had nothing but each other, and that pitiful place that we could barely heat, yet somehow it felt as though we had it all. Our parents thought we were reckless when we took on that run-down place. More so when we refused their offers of help. But we met the world and its ills head-on, determined, and independent from all but each other. They claimed that they understood in the end, but you said, "I don't think they do". You always thought they had a look of people who felt they had somehow failed in their duty as parents. Maybe they meant it in a way that implied a sense of pride. You said that any pride belonged to us, and us alone, and that made us omnipotent.

Not that way now, it seems. Instead, we are fragile entities, like the finest crystal in the palms of inept and quivering hands. But strength may come from places we never knew existed within ourselves. Words of wisdom you wielded as weapons against a frightening world of tests and treatments and clinically perfumed corridors. Our love was the armour, and oh how it bore the brunt of burden and ardour. This is why we must fight the fear these moments bring; we must endure and keep each other safe.

I continue, onwards, my hand reaching for your arm, ready to help you reconnect with the world, *our* world that we have built from nothing but respect and dedication and loss and hope.

And as I reach, so too do I look upon the pane against which you tap, tap, tap.

Then I see her in the glass.

The woman's face has vacant eyes, lips moving soundlessly, and I am at once confused, unsure that such a thing should be there instead of you. Those eyes are distracted beyond knowing. So this is why you insist on tapping the glass. You are trying to gain her attention, to break through her trance, so she can explain how she can be there, and what it is she wants with us. I look to you, seeking confirmation on my theory. You are no longer there, but the tapping on the glass continues, and I frown.

Things were so different, once. Do you remember that time when you went away – some work thing or other, a conference in Cape Town – you had never been so far from home. We both felt the distance, the yearning to be back together. The term 'soulmates' was made for us, those two weeks proved the belief was not mere whimsy. You told me that you stood atop Table Mountain, watched the Indian and Atlantic oceans meet off Cape Point, the mass of light and dark green stitched from shore to horizon with a writhing thread of foam. Yet such a monumental moment was dulled in that we could not share it together. All I could think about was you, pining for me, and how I needed to embrace you, hold you close so you never felt that way again. The thought of that embrace brings with it warm waves of contentment, and I succumb to the riptide.

The woman in the window momentarily frowns, then a smile plays upon her lips, as though she is able to read my thoughts. Somehow it feels right that she should know, that she should want to do such a thing.

A hand rests lightly upon my arm, accompanied by a resigned and patient sigh. Why am I not afraid? Why does this make sense on one level and not on another? The woman in the glass reflects my dilemma with a puzzled expression of her own. Turning my head, I forego her bewilderment, my gaze on the hand placed upon my sleeve, moving then to the wrist and the forearm, stopping when I see a face etched with sadness and there are tears, glistening in the dimmed wall lights, and they traverse cheeks as pale as alabaster.

Is that you? How can you be there when you were just *here*, tapping the window, trying to get the attention of the woman in the glass? Is that why the tap, tap, tap is no longer on the air? Is such an action no longer needed because she has finally revealed her secrets and you somehow understand the whys and wherefores of who she is?

Despite your tears, there is a warm, albeit watery, smile. My emotions coalesce, and the confusion mounts. I am at once afraid and calmed, frustrated and content, and I tell you that I don't understand what is happening.

The smile garners strength and the hand upon my arm gives a gentle squeeze, showing that I am understood. Words now, earnest and inviting, as you steer me away from the window, that place of baffling reflection, back into the lounge. I listen intently as once confounded languages now form in my mind, and I try to make them relevant. The conversion from bemusement to understanding is like wading through molasses. But it is worth it. Oh, yes. Comprehension finally comes after much fumbling and tumbling. My heart lifts, as do the corners of my mouth.

The hand on my arm now lifts and delicately sweeps strands of hair from my brow before placing a gentle palm upon my cheek. And there you are, eyes looking into mine, as though you are back at that window, seeking out the woman in the glass. And when your words come again, this time there is no struggle to make sense of them. And they are soft and sad yet forever hopeful.

"Things were so different, once. Do you remember?"

Last Rose of Summer

Her beauty consumes. A hungry animal; a sighing, sated heart. A million and one metaphors as to how she feeds the growing obsession.

Need?

Want?

Crave?

All these things and more as I watch her svelte, lithe frame traverse the shop, moving with poise and grace amongst brogue, sandal and boot, the way her paisley top clings to the small swell of her breasts, the flatness of her stomach, the pert peach sway of her buttocks, gift wrapped in a tight skirt and the blackest of woollen stockings.

"Can I help you, Sir?"

Her voice is soft, young. The badge on her chest tells me what I already know.

Rose Delaware: Sales Assistant.

"That's good of you," I say. "I'm looking for a new pair of loafers."

"You've come to the right place," she replies, giving me the kind of smile that comes with the salary. False, the product of a training course. I've seen it too many times. I own a mirror after all.

"What size?"

"Ten."

"Colour?"

"Burgundy."

The colour of long dead blood.

She nods and walks away from me, heading for the storeroom. I watch her, savour her; imagine her body bucking beneath me as I rob it of life.

I discretely adjust my trousers with a hand in a pocket.

After a few moments Rose is back, her black bobbed hair is a contrast to her skin, smooth and porcelain-pale. My monochrome muse kneels at my feet, pushing the fringe from her ice blue eyes, tucking it behind her right ear, where a scar shaped as a sickle smiles up at me. Inside I return its amity. And wonder if she weeps when she comes.

She will, of course. Maybe not at the beginning, when she's disorientated by the hood and the chloroform. But maybe when she feels her bonds, tight and secure about her wrists and ankles. Maybe at the realisation that she is naked, her flesh goosed by the cool breeze coming in through the warehouse window, her sex exposed and shaved, nipples so taut they crinkle. But weep she will. They always do, at the end, either pleading for life or begging for death, they always weep. It saddens me for a while, the sound of it, but then it irritates, gives the unreasoned beast reason to surface, to feed. And when it begins to chow down, it doesn't stop until insides are outside and the bright red splashes arc in the air like scarlet fireworks sent to the heavens.

"Would you like to walk in them?"

I look up. My pretty Rose is standing now, her smile indifferent. She does not know me. But later she will come to know me very well, she will no longer be indifferent, she will whisper my name over and over, blood and semen coating her throat.

"Sir?"

She appears irritated. I like that, a little fire in which to temper my steel.

"Yes, I shall walk in them."

I go through the motions, a charade in which the outside world will see a man trying on shoes, a non-descript man, a man who has layers of artifice beneath which he hides. An expensive wig, a moustache that will be shaven off with the same razor that will later remove Rose Delaware's pubic hair.

The same razor that will put a smile on her throat.

"These will do nicely," I say.

I sit back down. My performance done.

The world is not a stage; it's a hunting ground where the clothing of sheep will forever hide the wolf. And this wolf likes his clothes very much, takes comfort from the false fleece that allows safe passage through a world where morality marauds unchecked.

"They're a fine shoe," Rose says. "The finest Italian leather. Special occasion?"

"Yes."

I shall wear them tonight where they will be slick with your blood.

"Yes, very special."

"I'll pack them for you."

With care, of course. Not as the beast will later dispose of her after he lies sated and spent, bundling his Rose into bins bags, severed and separate, ready for burial. An arduous but necessary task, tidying the spoils.

The spoilt.

The beast has risen twelve times this summer. The same in previous years; never greedy, never hurried. Just like the time spent with my twelve beautiful red Roses. Miss Delaware is to be the last Rose of summer. Today, the beast will sow its seed and consume the crop. Then, it will sleep.

But summer comes so fast, doesn't it? The beast lies dormant, a bear in a deep, dark cave, waiting for the spring. The restlessness begins at the start of the year. New Year's Eve, that time when a year gone-by is wiped clean, alcohol washing it away along with accrued sin. Yet as others revel, I plan. A new town, a new city, a new virtual-phone book. So many Roses it is always difficult to choose. But choice is part of the ritual, part of the awakening. They are always young, always ripe for reaping, and when my twelve Roses are selected then they are cultivated, ready for the beast to turn them red

"There y'go," Rose gives me another faux grin. Her teeth, small and white and perfect, are framed in small pouting lips. Later they will be smashed out with a rubber mallet and stacked inside her navel.

She offers me the bag containing the shoes.

"Thank you, Miss," I say taking it from her, the bag creaking like something in need of oil.

Then I leave the shop, crossing the grey street teeming with dull figures and finding a coffee house. I settle down for a latte with a duplo espresso and an onion bagel with creamed cheese. I stare at the shoe shop opposite, my booth a haven from the hubbub about me. I will leave this place of solace in twenty minutes. Rose will leave the store in twenty five, her shift behind her and an evening of unforeseen pain ahead.

She will walk to her car, a small thing with metallic blue paint, highly polished with an immaculate interior, the hallmarks of redundant weekends and a life on her own. And as she walks to her metallic blue chariot, bouncing a key ring that is more ring than key in her delicate hands, I will wait with the rag and the hood and the promise that tonight will not be a night she has to spend without company.

I check my watch, an expensive piece that keeps good time. My only luxury, keeping good time. For beautiful Rose it is a commodity that is running out. Like clear water pouring from a desert well. Soon it will be dry.

And Rose will be defiled and dead.

I leave the shop, and make my way west, pre-emptively following Rose's route. I sense the tension around me; see the people moving with purpose across the urban landscape. I see them as indiscernible shapes, shadows in a fog of obsession. But I can almost taste their fear. They have purpose, and that purpose is to go home, the place instinct equates with safety and comfort.

The banner headline on the newspaper stand suggests otherwise.

White Orchid Kills Again! Woman slaughtered in her own home!

White Orchid.

Somewhere inside the beast stirs. It is not its time, so I pet it, placate it. And, for now, it returns to its restless slumber. The city has two predators, yet only one has celebrity. White Orchid is sensationalist, leaving his work for all to see. There is no subtlety. The kills are left in their homes, nailed to chairs, to walls, to headboards. A single white orchid jammed and blossoming from their open mouths. It is the act of someone craving notoriety, not the way of someone taking pride in their work. And like thirsty dogs the press lap it up, giving the ultimate accolade, a monstrous moniker for the public to whisper when they are alone in the dark.

White Orchid.

I balk at such a thing. It cheapens the craft. And the MO is slovenly, White Orchid claiming men and women, young and old alike.

No precision. No calibre.

I make my way to the car park. It has three storeys and CCTV. In the public toilets en route, I remove a layer of artifice, to expose another. The wig is discarded in the cistern, the cistern filled with bleach tablets, the horsehair fizzing and hissing like a huge guinea pig in a sea of fat. And like the moth from the pupae, I emerge from the toilets as something different. Most will see a man, but beneath lurks the monster, pensive and patient, in tune with the hunt.

Rose Delaware moves through the car park, the pillars throwing black blocks of shadow onto grey tarmac, her pale skin turning ashen as she courts the darkness. I become fascinated by her legs, athletic, yet not too muscular, but supple. It is a good sign. Her hips may not dislocate as she struggles against her bonds. These things happen sometimes. It matters not to the beast, though the screams can be tiresome. They can detract from the enjoyment of an event, like a wasp at a barbeque. Or forgetting to bring your favourite knife; the one with the razor's edge that opens deep canyons in taut flesh.

A sound to my right.

The chime of the elevator. It has big, dull doors that peel apart to reveal its innards, a silver car for those laden with too much shopping or too much body weight to use the stairs from the mall beneath. I skulk into the shadows, use them, become them.

Movement.

A figure steps from the elevator car, the doors now patient and silent. A man, a big man, wearing an expensive suit. The warm breeze circulating through the car park brings aftershave mingling with the diesel. His scent.

In his hands, the newcomer carries a box. It is garish and has a motif that is too small to see from my hiding place.

Then he is moving and there is something in his stride that concerns me. Each step is different, one hesitant, the other brisk, as though someone is battling with the decision of which pace to use. I have seen it before, back in the early days when I was a novice. Trying to maintain control over the excitement, trying to keep the beast leashed.

My heart, a slow calculating thing, picks up pace. This is no man. This is a predator. And he is here to make claim on my prize. As he passes me, I see the box up close, confirming what I already know. The motif is that of a flower, a silhouette with three broad leaves and a coned tuba rising like a vase. The motif is white.

A white orchid.

I nod with resignation, and feel my face contort into quiet rage. White Orchid has opted to pluck my Rose from the Earth. The beast is now awake and has something to say about it, but it is still chained, unable to be allowed the kind of liberty that would have it gripping and gouging, stamping and snapping, with a howl in its throat. Rose is *mine*. She is the last of this summer and I will not be denied. This appeases the beast. It lies down as if to resume its nap, but this time its eyes remain open.

I take a breath and do what I do best. I watch. I calculate. Assess how this will go. White Orchid will not nail my Rose to a concrete pillar in a city car park. He will subdue her somehow and take her back to the small flat she has in the city suburbs. A flat with five rooms and an air of solitude.

Rose is nearing her car when she sees him. I feel my muscles pull taut. I can be on him in seconds should he choose to kill her here. Yet I know that even the sensationalist in him will not allow for getting caught. It is clear that he enjoys his work too much to retire so soon.

My Rose looks up and her face, pale and pretty, changes. Not to surprise or fear. Instead, it smiles, and her eyes become doe-like and coquettish, blinking rapidly as though battling tears.

"Hello, you," she says. Her voice is quiet and tremulous. "This is a pleasant surprise."

"I just had to see you, Rose," the man replies. He has a rich and resonant tone. I'm unsure if this is natural or enhanced by the high ceilings about us. "I had to see you in the flesh."

"You couldn't wait until eight?" Her smile is bright, fuelled by his faux flattery. At least I now know how he intends to subdue her. Not with violence but with seduction, the oldest form of entrapment. I relax with the knowledge. He will woo her; then take her home.

And I shall follow.

"You brought it?" she is saying, her head nodding to indicate the box in his hands.

"I said I would." White Orchid offers the box, and she takes it gingerly. "Just in case you didn't recognise me."

"It's beautiful."

"So are you," White Orchid feigns embarrassment very well. "Your avatar really doesn't do you justice," he finishes.

I watch my Rose flush, her cheeks becoming twin plumes of fire, increasing in their intensity as White Orchid leans down and plants a kiss on her brow. I watch her thighs squeeze together as she fights the tingle that is awakening her sex.

I stamp on the green-eyed monster threatening to maul the beast within. White Orchid, it seems, is not as I'd envisaged.

Rose plays with the box. "Must've been tough to get one of these. I'll admit I didn't think you'd do it. I'm sorry I didn't believe you."

"You don't know me," White Orchid replies holding up a placating hand. "We all have problems with trust, right? That's why we use the agency."

Dating agency. Slick. My intrigue is growing. Maybe I misjudged White Orchid. No need for harsh chemicals or a cosh to the neck, just a few kind words to those who aren't used to hearing them. No novice here, I now realise. Instead, a smooth operator, a sophisticated killing machine. I admire all except his choice of target.

I may regret having to kill him. But needs must when the monster drives.

"I hope to know you a little more after tonight," Rose says, her eyes coy beneath her fringe. The flush is still there but fading. She is growing confident in his presence. She is taking the bait. Soon Rose will be in the trap, torn and bloody.

I take my eyes away from the scene for a few moments; search the car park for my van. It is dark and inconspicuous, the plates false, as much a lie as its current owner, and as such destined to disappear as effectively as the dismembered remains it will carry later this evening. My ride is several spaces away from Rose's vehicle.

"The table is booked for eight thirty," White Orchid says.

"What if I told you that I'm not hungry?" Rose replies. I watch as she gives White Orchid a playful, knowing smile. I see her tongue flit across her lips and the big man leans down again to push it back into her mouth with his own.

For a moment I am lost. I see his hands cup one of her buttocks, caressing it, kneading it until his fingers grow bored and slip down to the hem of her skirt, his hand a pink, five legged spider traversing to her thigh, where it stays for a while.

Then I hear it, the sound of silky pleasure escaping from Rose's throat, her mouth still working on the kiss. A quiet, subtle sound that will ensure that Rose Delaware will become another of White Orchid's trophies.

I know that I must stay focused in order to stay in the game. Otherwise, he will claim her. I am mesmerised as the two finally separate their faces.

"Shall we go to your place?" White Orchid asks.

"I spend enough time in my place. Can't we go somewhere else?" Rose's voice is breathless with lust.

But I'm more surprised by White Orchid's response to her request. Again, he thwarts my expectations. I expect him to suggest otherwise, to get clumsy and make up some excuse as to why they should go back to Rose's cold, emotionless flat.

Instead, he nods. "We could go to my place?"

"I'd like that," she says. "Do you have your car here?"

"I came by train."

"This is my car. Direct me."

She activates her remote key fob and the door locks pop on her car. It is a dead sound. I feel it is apt considering the pending fate of its owner.

Rose climbs in after putting the box containing the white orchid onto the back seat. The killing machine called White Orchid then sits beside her. I see him place a hand on her thigh just before her door shuts me out.

The engine fires first time and Rose reverses out of the parking space. The car waits a moment as the two of them kiss again, then it pulls away, its taillights blood red, a terrible portent of things to come.

I have to cover ground quickly if I am to not lose sight of White Orchid. I'm in my van within moments, but my actions are not frantic. Despite the increasing clamour of the beast, the cold computer in my head continues to calculate, plotting what must be done. Panic will not resolve this matter, only determination and the absolute certainty that Rose Delaware will have no one inside her tonight but me. My sex, my hands, my Italian leather loafers, she will have them all.

I begin the hunt.

I keep my distance, allowing two cars to stack between the van and Rose's car, my elevated position keeping the metallic blue shimmer in sight. I'm aware that at the car park exit there is a "right turn only" sign that will lead Rose into the city. I won't lose them; the one way system will be my ally for a good few miles.

On the street the night is making itself known, blackness nuzzling against the city skyline. Streetlamps have woken, their sodium flare in competition with the multifarious sidelights of vehicles clogging the streets. We pass shops wrapping up for the night and those places that are about to open. Wanton places, the kind that attract creatures of the night. Places like the *Mucho Mojo Club*, creatures like *me*.

Rose is still two cars ahead. I'm adept at being incognito, a predatory chameleon, fuelled by caution and prowess. As the traffic thins out, I drop back, waiting for Rose's car to peel away from the city and into suburbia. It happens within ten minutes. Now there is only distance between my van and her taillights.

She takes a right turn. Then a left. Buildings are becoming both sparse and squat. I recognise it as a fledging exclusive estate, an elite ghetto that faces the river, giving extensive, executive views.

The car pulls to a stop at a gated entrance. I pull over, three hundred yards behind and watch as White Orchid gets out of the vehicle and types a code into a keypad bolted to the gate house.

My eyes scan the walls circumventing the incomplete luxury apartments. It is token, more a statement than a valid means of protection. It can be scaled easily, and I prove this once the taillights have crossed the threshold and the gates have clicked shut.

On foot I follow, a baseball cap for added anonymity from any potential CCTV cameras, keeping to the deep shadows cast by the buildings about me. There are few lights in the windows of the four storey buildings. Not all, it appears, have occupiers yet. I see Rose's car park up outside one of the smaller apartments. It has only two floors and is mostly dark; the sign outside suggesting that it is part apartment, part show home. I guess this is White Orchid's cover. The consummate salesman making the ultimate deal. I hunker down and wait, my breathing slow, steady. A light comes on in a ground floor window, a rectangle of yellow, quartered by its frame. I move quickly, time now a more pressing enemy. I make it to the foyer, a compact space furnished with a small sofa and an abandoned reception desk. In future times I'm sure it will manned by a man on minimum wage, now it is but a show piece, a façade that, like the perimeter wall, offers little security.

The computer in my brain has already identified a means of escape once I have secured my Rose, saved her from one kind of death only to introduce her to another. Her car will become the Trojan horse, I will subdue White Orchid, the beast making short work of him. Then Rose will be grateful, will come to me and in a moment of trust, I shall make her mine. She will move from apartment to car boot and then to the van, where the night can truly begin.

The corridor ahead has four doors, two embedded in each wall. Three of the four have "for sale" labels slapped upon surfaces of rich mahogany. The fluorescents overhead are hidden behind ornate, frosted glass, but the light is low wattage, casting a gossamer motif on the walls and floor. In the stillness I hear the delicate tinkle of glass and a loud thump. It is a sound I can place in an instant: the sound of a body hitting the floor. And it has come from behind the door without a label.

White Orchid works fast. Again, I have misjudged him, the beast inside curses me for my complacency.

I stride towards the door, hoping beyond hope that my Rose isn't too damaged. My palm encapsulates the brass handle just as the first scream slices through the air.

It is high pitched, the sound of someone in great pain. No, not pain, agony. I can hear another noise, the rhythmic metallic chime of hammer against nail.

White Orchid is working hard on Rose. The beast within can be contained no longer, it knows its prey is in danger of being wrestled away, sullied and spoilt.

I lift a foot. It meets mahogany, the force of the blow taking the door off its frame with a harsh, splintering crash.

Inside the apartment all the lights blaze. There is opulence here, leather and crystal and chrome. But all pale in significance next to the blood. It has pooled in plate-sized patches, seeping into the lush white carpets. It splashes against the walls like some macabre abstract painting. Even the beast is quelled by its beauty, and the sight of the thing in the room. The thing that was once a person, but is now nailed to the floor, through the wrists, the feet, the groin.

Its mouth remains open, the scream no longer high pitched since the vocal cords have been expertly severed, so that only a bubbling hiss remains rising into the air as a fine red mist. And the white orchid is now out of the box and jammed in the thing's mouth.

The beast salivates, but the computer calculates. Then it draws its conclusions.

The thing nailed to the floor of the apartment isn't Rose Delaware. It is White Orchid. But no sooner do I realise this than I also recognise that I have once more misjudged the other predator holding this city in its maw.

My red Rose is White Orchid.

I cannot help but smile with the knowledge of it, even as a shadow falls across me, and I feel the needle sting of a hypodermic in my neck. My muscles collapse under the influence of a powerful anaesthetic.

Rose stands over me, still beautiful, yet now I see her for what she truly is: brutal and brilliant.

"I've been waiting for you." Her smile is sweet poison upon her lips, her eyes travel down to my brand new loafers. "I see you wore them."

I try to nod, but the attempt is as token as her interest.

We are kindred. And I know that as I look upon her, I have been no expert hunter and she no hapless prey. While my eyes have stared at her back, hers have been on me throughout, sprinkling breadcrumbs for a witless, eager child to follow. I am clay, manipulated in her masterful hands, every moment I thought she was in my sights, I have been standing in her trap. I am a puppet, and the sharp tools she has at her disposal are sure to be cutting more than just my strings.

Soon I shall begin screaming as she gives me her love. And through it all, my Rose does indeed weep. But her tears are not those of sorrow or regret or fear.

They are the sparkling jewels of pure, absolute joy.

Masquerade

I was ripped from the Earth, screaming.

Mouth wide, soul torn, my agony doomed to an infinite silence. In the darkness, in the flicker flash of lightning, in the ferocity of flame, I remember the screaming and the cursing and, yes, the begging for forgiveness, I remember that too. Yet such was my penance, such was the very sin with which I had cloaked my life, there was no respite from the torment. No reprieve from the punishment hanging about my ethereal neck like a yoke of serpents, biting, biting, biting; paralysing what little flesh remained upon my cursed carcass and poisoning a mind that had long since tried to take its leave.

But I would not go mad. Not for long. No splendid isolation here in this brutal netherworld, no madness to anaesthetise the suffering. No, The Paymaster made sure I was lucid enough to endure its retribution. It didn't want me to miss the point, after all, the *purpose* of my stint in purgatory. So I went through the branding and the cutting and the tearing and gouging, unseen demons feeding as a trapped, starving dog would savage its long dead master.

And just when there was nothing left, just when I thought I would finally cease to exist, the whole thing would start over, slowly, deliberately, my cries and frustrations yielding only mocking laughter from the darkness.

But that was then. Before the awareness.

Before the *awakening*.

~

It starts as though I'm waking from a terrible dream. Consciousness is returning, an old friend cold and damp from a spell in the wilderness. It's a good thing, a welcome thing. Like cool rain after a savage heat. Now there is no darkness, only grey. And in this twilight, I see things that are at once familiar.

And not.

I left behind many things, before the screaming. Material memories: a house, a business, vast wealth; a handsome frame that lured the wanton and the weak. That was my vice, back in the days when I was a man. But the trappings of success were never enough. I was flawed; ever plagued by the sense that something was missing. My heart: a vacuum, a functional organ to merely perpetuate the misery.

Misery!

As if I knew what that word really meant back then. But in reality, I know the thing I craved never existed in the first place. The feeling of belonging was as much a fallacy as a desert mirage to those with a frantic thirst. But I'd sought it so long, so often, using all means at my disposal to find the one thing lacking in my old existence.

Happiness.

The drugs, the booze, the sex, all props in a B-movie lifestyle, coupled with me, the ultimate bad actor. And where I stand in death is testament to the wholesale failure to attain it in life. The money bought more than just luxury, it bought guidance, the darkest kind, the kind that skulks in shadows, or is whispered by people crippled by superstition and age. The kind in which the desperate draw hope.

I was advised against the path I'd chosen to take, of course. But arrogance and the need for peace became armour against a barrage of fair warnings. I paid a king's ransom to make the warnings go away, to disappear like the ghost I was destined to become. And allowed the rituals to take place, using darkness to find the light missing from my life.

They began in the basement, specially prepped, and daubed with symbols which I couldn't recognise, let alone understand. And, as the mysterious employee I found in a murky area of the Dark web painted them onto the walls, they appeared to glow, as though branded into the brickwork. When I should have seen nothing but folly, I found hope. And so began my downfall. With the symbols and the chanting and the rituals came that which I had craved far more than money. I was full, brimming over where before I was barren. I had fire in my belly, a euphoria that opened doors upon the world. I could see my achievements, became overwhelmed by them, the sense of pride almost intoxicating.

But with happiness came the blindness. Not in a literal sense, that may have ultimately been more difficult to overlook. Or ignore.

No, I became blind to the chaos such newly found rapture was creating about me. Decadence became my companion; debauchery, my friend. I sampled all the delights that I could acquire, of the flesh, of the mind. Money was no barrier. In fact, I was fast becoming a fiscal paradox. The more money I frittered away, the more I made. And as I scaled the heights of depravity, so I created the pit destined to claim me.

But I didn't realise the real price of gaining Nirvana until later, when it was time to settle the bill. The Paymaster came for me in late October, when the world was sleeping, and I was engaged in another night of wanton lust. It came as fire, bright searing flame that at once scorched my skin, crisping it, clogging my nostrils with the stench of roasting meat, filling my ears with the sound of hissing and spitting fat.

My companions at the time, three models and a girl I'd met during a particularly good party, watched as I cavorted about the room, screaming in an agony that would become my tailor in the lifetime of purgatory awaiting me. Their faces were coke and booze-fuelled masks; one of the models, a petite thing with huge breasts and small nipples, even told me to stop fucking around.

The Paymaster was for my eyes only; I knew it even in the searing, frying heat. In that moment, it told me of the crimes I had committed in the pursuit of happiness, and now it was time to dig deep.

And it took my yelling, yammering soul with it to the doors of oblivion, and cast them wide, where, for the next aeon (but for mortal men: mere moments) I paid my dues, as the cash registers chimed in time with my screams.

~

"Where do we start?"

The voice is loud, almost too loud. It bites deeply into what was once my brain, now just matter ripe for persecution. The grey fog before me becomes translucent, gossamer glass that suddenly lets in the world from which I'm now disparate.

A woman appears, peering right through me; not difficult given my current standing, though I sense this is something else. The way a person courts vanity in a window made of one way glass, checking themselves out though unaware that someone unknown is joining in, and perhaps enjoying a better view.

The woman is fine looking. Green eyes in almond frames, long lashes flitting like the delicate wings of a butterfly. Her olive skin is unblemished, her neck slim and marred only by the ebony strands that have escaped the scrunchie holding the rest of her hair in situ.

I watch as this beautiful, delicate creature leans forward and checks herself over, a slim finger pressing and pulling at the taut flesh of her cheeks.

"Where are the years going, Emily?" the woman says looking right at me.

I have no answer.

The finger that had been exploring Emily's face reaches out towards me, and I shiver, my phantom loins stirring after an eternity of slumber. It is a shockingly delicious sensation. The finger stops short, as though Emily is pointing directly at me, an accusation, an awareness of my presence. Of my sin. Yet I see the fingertip expand as though hitting something solid, the diaphanous barrier between worlds. She rubs at something unseen, and then withdraws her hand.

"Must give it a clean," she sighs. "Maybe it'll improve the view."

A mirror separates us.

I realise this almost as immediately as the notion that this is not meant to be happening.

Somehow, this little event is going on under the purgatory radar. The darkness, it seems, is no-one's ally here in the belly of the netherworld.

Emily stands and I now see all, as her self-critique extends to her body. It is slim, perhaps slightly too thin in places: her belly, for example, where it sinks slightly, evident even beneath her silken night dress. Her legs are long, the hem of her nightwear tantalisingly short, revealing most of her thighs. As she turns, the hem becomes my friend and allows a glimpse of one of her buttocks, and the thread of a white thong.

She holds this position and looks over her shoulder, looks straight at me, but instead sees a bigger disappointment.

"How could anyone love *that*?" Her voice is taut with frustration and she spins and slumps back before me in one fluid movement. A sulk sets up camp in her face, and I wonder why she cannot see what I see: an image of elegance and beauty that should melt hearts, break them, and have them begging for her to accept their love for eternity.

Maybe she has something missing?

The ethereal thought is there before I can register it as my own. Yes, what if this corporeal goddess, this slice of heaven on Earth, is one of the unfortunate who, like me, had it all but saw nothing, felt nothing, but an endless vacuous parasite sucking the joy out of life?

At once I feel her despair, her emptiness. We have affinity. We have...

What?

What do we have that suddenly and assuredly means something? We have *connection*. A tether transcending the planes in which we find ourselves, an unholy umbilical that has the potential to free us both.

For the first time in this period of reprieve, I feel fear. Would The Paymaster be aware if I begin to plot? To hope? Would my chance to be free of this endless world of torment be ripped from me, as my soul had been from the Earth? I do not want to be cast in the role of a parasite. I want to be a saviour; to create a symbiosis that could connect with the girl. I want to breach the barrier and give her the things she really craves. Empower her eyes to actually see who she is and what the world owes her.

Us.

"I'm useless," Emily says and her smooth shoulders sag under the weight of her conclusion. I want to take hold of those shoulders, and draw her to me, make her mine, body and soul, and in return I will give her the world as she's never considered it before. A world in which she is special and all who look upon her are ensnared by her grace and splendour. And all I would ask in return is that she accept me as her conscience and facilitates my freedom. And my price? Only that Emily allows me to wear her face, to use her oh-so-exquisite body.

But how? How can I make this happen? How do I bridge worlds and occupy another's thoughts?

The notion is fleeting because no sooner is it there than my consciousness is nudging at the translucent membrane separating us, and for a moment the barrier yields, but then it is a solid mass once more, resistant to my endeavours.

Frustrated, I cry out, and immediately admonish my recklessness. The Paymaster may hear and return with the chains and the hooks and the red hot knives. Moments pass and nothing changes, the pain and suffering does not return. At least, not for now.

I watch Emily dab her eyes with a tissue. She's knocked over a bottle of perfume in the process and is cursing under her breath, her voice hitching. Then she stands and moves away from the mirror, and immediately I mourn the loss of her company. She wanders to the other side of the room where a four-poster bed receives her.

Lying on her side, facing the mirror, she balls up her small fists and pushes them against her eye sockets as if attempting to stem the twin cataracts coursing down her cheeks. She is mostly successful, though some tear drops still escape and traverse unchecked, dampening the huge white pillow. She epitomises a soul in misery, as tormented in her reality as I am in mine.

I continue to watch her sobbing against the duck down and linen, listening to her melancholy sighs until sleep embraces her. As Emily's small breasts rise and fall in rhythm with her slumber, I suddenly become aware that the barrier between us begins to shimmer, no longer impenetrable but a shifting, undulating wall of silver against which I instinctively press.

And pass through.

I feel the atmosphere punch through my spirit, buffeting me as though I'm being swept away by cascading, turbulent waters of an invisible river. For a few seconds I am disorientated, turned upwards, smashed downwards, harsh noises in my ears roar like angry, hungry beasts.

Then I adapt. Consciousness plays no part in it; equilibrium appears to happen, the natural and supernatural deciding to get along for a while. I am the air, I am the dust motes and mites, drifting across the room, drawn to my beautiful Emily the way a moth is pulled inexorably to a winking porch light. The surge of excitement as I near this wonderful creature intoxicates, it leaves me reeling, and the thought of this moment being snatched away before I can connect with her is more painful than anything I have endured at the hands of The Paymaster's minions.

In her sleep Emily rolls over onto her back, the nightdress riding upwards and exposing her delicate white underwear. I hover above her, staring longingly at this sleeping beauty destined to soon become the vessel in which I shall plot my escape. As though in agreement, a small 'yes' escapes from her lips. I realise she is dreaming, and I know with certainty it is through her dreams that I am allowed to be free of my torment. She is searching for a liberator, and I shall heed her call. I descend, rest upon her and sink down, our minds and bodies fusing. My consciousness weeps with the joy of it. Emily lets out a long sigh.

Just as my escape from the mirror triggered a barrage of senses, so does my melding with Emily. At once I see her past and her present, experience them as if they are my own. Here come the doubts and the fears and the self-loathing. They arrive like savage, rabid dogs eager to feast upon the promise I bring. But they are no match. I rise above them and bring about their ruin. Emily has a new champion, a soulless saviour destined to steer her towards a different life in a much bigger world.

After moments we are one, our bodies entwined like copulating lovers, our minds fused, yet my consciousness will always dominate at times of doubt. No more the wallflower. Soon Emily will be smashing through the brick and stones of her own prison and tasting the sweet air of liberty.

She (we) stare towards the mirror, eyes suddenly open. I (she) smiles at her image across the room, as if seeing herself through my eyes, understanding that she is at once a sight to behold, and the world is hers for the taking.

I encourage her to celebrate, revere her newfound confidence. I take one of her small hands to her left breast, where the soft movements of her palm create hungry pleasure. The other hand travels sedately down her flat stomach until it stops where she yearns for its touch. Her fingers oblige, teasing, probing, each gentle movement causing her to let go small sighs that begin to grow in time, until her body seems to buckle under the pressure of it all, her back arching like a cat who has espied something unseen, and the coarse high pitched cry explodes into the room as my Emily finds release.

She lies there, gasping, the hand that had brought her so much pleasure covering her mouth to stifle a giggle of disbelief.

"What would mother have said?" she says to the room.

Mother probably did the same.

My thought is her thought. And as such she accepts it. We are one. Connection: complete.

So begins the masquerade. I steer Emily through the house I left behind. The layout is as I know it, but it is full of her things, her tastes. But no matter, it is early days, after all. We shall rethink the pastel décor, revisit the crystal vases and the bone china. They are things of grace, admittedly, but they are the tastes of the sedate and pedestrian. Emily is her mother's daughter, that is clear. It is this matriarch against which this young passionate woman has gauged her life; love and respect have become a ball and chain.

Time for the bolt cutter.

We go to the kitchen and Emily opens the door to the refrigerator and removes a soda. She pops the lid and takes several deep swallows. I feel the fizzing liquid gurgle down her gullet, wince along with her as the brain freeze hits and grin as the sugar kicks in.

Go on, let it out.

The belch is long and loud and unrestrained. Emily gets a fit of the giggles when she's done and inside, I laugh along. This is pleasure after my mini lifetime of despair. The opportunities for us are, of course, far more than simple pleasures of the flesh and puerile soda farts. This masquerade will have no limits, no fetter to hold it or restrain its horizons.

"I can't believe I'm doing this," Emily says.

I assume she means her newfound rebellion against convention, or her wholesale murder of mediocrity. Instead, she moves out of the kitchen and towards the hall. It has high ceilings and is dear to my heart. I remember it as the place where I once received news that I had made another fortune and for the first time felt genuine happiness. The high chandelier is still there. At the moment it is dark, its opulence muted.

Emily passes through the hall and down towards another door.

"I really can't believe you're doing this."

We say it in unison. For I recognise her intention. And balk with sudden and assured fear.

Ahead is the door to the basement. The basement where there are symbols glowing like brands in the brickwork. We share the fear. We both have our memories of the place, after all. And Emily's come swiftly, a torrent of them, slapping into me, almost bowling me over in their urgency to introduce themselves.

~

"And this is the basement, Miss Kain," a middle aged estate agent with an expensive suit and a cheap pitch is saying. His eyes roam over Emily's body when she's not looking. Later that day he will masturbate with the image of Emily's buttocks in his head. "Not for the squeamish, I must add."

"What do you mean?" Emily of memories replies.

"Well, there's a rumour that something most *unpleasant* happened to the previous owner," the estate agent smiles, relishing the tale. "They say he went mad. Painted symbols on the walls and dabbled in what some would call *black magic*."

"That sounds quite scary." Emily's recollections portray her as a timid yet neat woman, her face a mask of uncertainty. "What happened to him?"

"Disappeared," the estate agent whispers, his eyes gleaming.

"Oh."

"All nonsense, of course," the man says quickly. "The musings of idle minds."

"Of course," Emily says, the love of the house – *my* house – overriding the estate agent's spiel. But the story of my demise has remained with her, keeping her away from the basement, her mind filling in blanks and fostering fear.

Until now.

It seems I have created a paradox. Emily's lust for touting taboos has extended to the basement. I swallow my terror the way Emily swallowed her soda, and gently suggest that she ceases this ridiculous idea.

What if something's down there?

That halts her steps, but not for long. To my horror Emily shakes her head and laughs.

"Don't be so stupid," she admonishes. "That's something Mother would say."

Maybe we could listen to Mother, just as a one off?

I try to stop Emily reaching for the basement door. I fail. Her hands clutch at latch, lifting it, and she yanks the door wide.

A breeze gooses her skin, but for me it is a raging gale made up of the cries of the damned.

Don't do this, Emily!

She steps over the threshold and leans in, probing fingers searching for the light switch. A bulb comes on. It is low wattage, made dimmer by a sheath of dust.

She takes a breath and makes her way down a flight of wooden steps laced with cobwebs. I am frozen. My very soul is trapped in a mitt of fear.

Then I see them.

The symbols line the far wall as Emily gets to ground level. And yes, they still glow, but this time their meanings are no longer alien, they are as clear as the agony I have endured for a thousand lifetimes.

Since I cannot control my Emily, I decide that I must abandon her, take my chances this side of the mirror, rather than risk being dragged back to Hell. I writhe and struggle to try and break free, but no sooner do I start this protest than I know it is doomed to fail. Because we are no longer alone in the basement.

HE is here.

The Paymaster, his face hidden by layers of skin, my own flesh, flayed from my screaming carcass as the demons jeered and cackled and masturbated. His eyes are the pits of Hell, without presence or pity, but the smile – the leer – says all.

Caught.

The Paymaster moves towards Emily. He is swathed in a bodice of thorns and harsh spikes that carve vicious weals into his flesh. But I know this creature enjoys pain almost as much as it loves inflicting it. He is fuelled by it, relishes it. He reaches out to Emily, and I know she does not see him, as I know that he has no interest in her.

His fingers are twisted twigs of ravaged tissue, and unbeknownst to her, they reach into Emily's chest, taking hold of my wriggling and struggling soul, singeing it, crushing it, welcoming me home.

And so, it is back, a high pitched, soaring, mind numbing sound, a sound that has been my soundtrack for lifetimes.

The cry of agony, absolute.

Cries punctuated by the hideous guffaws of The Paymaster, mouth a warped 'O', pieces of his (my) flesh mask slopping onto the floor at the ferocity of it. And somewhere between the horror and the agony I finally see what he wants me to see, that this entire masquerade is his doing, possession and re-possession. A cycle of retribution akin to the ritual torture endured for eternity. Slightly different, of course, for this goes far deeper, this gets beneath the layers and into the very core of my soul, ripping it open, exposing it to the world.

"Time to return," The Paymaster hisses.

And from the dark shadows of the basement his minions slink joyously out, their knives and chains and tools of torture clattering in their wake.

~

I was ripped from the Earth, screaming...

Where There's a Will...

The beige walls corralled a room that was small and sparsely furnished. On the air, a heavy smell of surgical spirit and detergent did not mask the quiet and insistent odour of urine. Its sweet, acrid aroma lingered like a ghost.

In the heavy stillness, the man on the bed whispered, the words rising from his shivering lips lost to the young woman sitting next to him. After turning down the corner of the page, Nurse Amanda Softly placed the book she'd been reading on the bedside locker. Adjusting the black cardigan draped over the shoulder of her white uniform, Amanda reached out for the man's gnarled, aged hand and gently covered it with her own. Her skin was marble-smooth, and a stark contrast to the wizened hand it now encapsulated.

"Hush, now, Arthur," she said gently. "Be at peace."

If Arthur Conlon heard her words, there was no acknowledgement. He continued his muted monotone ramblings, sallow face made fat by a dirty grey beard. This was what Alzheimer's disease did to its host, a dirty parasite sucking dry the faculties of man and leaving an empty vessel to drift through life rudderless, incapable of thought or memory.

"How is he?"

Despite its softness, Amanda was startled by the voice.

She looked up, her brown eyes meeting those of the man now standing at the foot of Arthur's bed. He was clad in the garb of a male orderly. Indeed, he even had a clip board under his right arm and a biro tucked behind his left ear.

For a moment, Amanda's brain told her she had never seen the man before, but within seconds of thinking such a thing, her mind shimmied and she suddenly felt giddy enough to sit back down and bring a palm up to her brow. The vertigo passed as soon as it came, and when she once more eyed the orderly, Amanda believed she'd known him for seven years and that he went by the name of Dan Murphy.

"Hi, Dan," she said tentatively. "I'm afraid he's not long for this world."

"I suspect not. We are all just passing through, after all," Dan replied, his voice almost whimsical. He had bright blue eyes and, even in the low light from her reading lamp, they sparkled like black ice in the winter sun. "I've come to relieve you."

"Is it that time already?" She yawned before he could answer and realised it probably *was* that time. "Strange how tiredness creeps up on you during a nightshift isn't it?" she sighed.

"Lots of things can creep around in the dark," Dan smiled. As he spoke his face appeared to shiver in the light, as though the table lamp did not contain a bulb at all, but a sputtering flame.

"Now don't you go saying things that will be giving me nightmares, Daniel Murphy," she said with a grin.

He laughed along with her, but had she looked closer she would have seen his mouth was not moving. Instead, it was a hyphen framed by dark lips.

Amanda stood and picked up her book. "I shall do the rounds and make us a nice cup of coffee. That sound good to you?"

"Wonderful," said Dan.

"How do you take it again?" Amanda asked. She couldn't quite recall having ever made coffee for Dan.

"As black as Lucifer's soul." He licked his lips, and Amanda blinked twice. Tiredness was playing tricks on her again. For a moment she thought that the tongue Dan had dragged across his teeth had been blue and *forked*.

She shook the image away and went out of the room, stopping in the doorway, her silhouette large and misshapen against the stark white corridor beyond.

"Please call me if he decides to pass on," she called.

Dan watched her go and looked down at the figure in the bed.

"Hello, Arthur," he said as he sat in Amanda's recently vacated chair. "Seems that your time's up."

~

The smile was back on Daniel's lips as he pulled the pen from behind his ear and placed the clip board on his knees.

Arthur continued to mutter incoherently, eyelids flickering fervently as though struggling to remain shut.

"If this is going to work, you really *are* going to have to speak up, dear fellow," Dan said.

He raised a hand, extending a finger which he placed on Arthur's forehead, and muttered under his breath, "Ego tribuo vos expedio in illa, vestri denique moments." *I give you clarity in these, your final moments.*

Where Dan's fingertip met the papery skin, darkness pooled like an oil spill, radiating outwards until it became the size of an old penny. As Dan took his finger away, the black blot faded to grey as it sank into the skin. Within a few moments it had disappeared completely.

Arthur's eyes snapped open, and he gasped as though someone had just given him bad news.

"Easy now, Arthur," Dan said calmly. "Don't want to stop that old ticker before we start, do we?"

"Where am I?" Arthur enquired, bemused and trembling.

Dan consulted his clip board. "Meadowsweet Care Home, apparently," he replied after a few seconds. "Not really interested in the details, if I'm honest."

His awakening had Arthur flustered. This was relayed through the old man's face, his jaw slack, eyes wide and frightened. Yet he still couldn't move his body. His limbs felt as though strong arms held him, forcing him into the thin, foam mattress.

"Who are you and what do you want from me?" he asked. Despite his fear, his voice was hard-edged.

"What I *want* we will get to, eventually," Dan said with a wink.

Arthur groaned and closed his eyes as if to try to undo what had been done to him. "Let me go! I need to rest."

"Not wanting to open with a cliché but there's *no rest for the wicked*, dear Arthur. It's why I'm here, after all."

"I don't understand," said Arthur with the total conviction of a man who *really* didn't.

"Now, here's the thing," Dan replied. "I really wouldn't expect you to, not yet at least. But I'm here on behalf of Dean."

"I don't recognise that name." The comment came too fast to be true.

"Oh, I get that, Arthur. Yes, I get that *plenty*. So does Dean. And that is why I'm sitting here beside you right now having this little tête-à-tête."

"Get out of here!" Arthur said angrily. "Nurse! Nurse!"

"Oh, what big lungs you have for an old fella," Dan said calmly. "All pointless. Amanda can't hear you. At the moment time is nothing to her. We're in a kind of bubble, locked in, if you prefer. This is all happening in the blink of an eye. In five minutes Nurse Softly will bring me coffee and you'll be as dead as Elvis."

"Why can't you just let me be?" Arthur moaned.

"Ah, deflection," Dan mused. "I gave you enough juice to buff up that rusty tin can of a brain of yours. So I know you remember the part where I mentioned Dean. I want you to say the name."

"I will not."

"Say it or I will make you piss fire," said Dan. The smile was in place, but his eyes were dancing with malevolence. "I'm told it's quite painful."

Before Alzheimer's disease crippled his mind, Arthur was known for his defiance in the same way he was known for his conceit. Both returned now, stoked by fear and anger at a past he'd rather remain unvisited.

"You're talking nonsense."

"Hmmm," Dan said, feigning thoughtfulness. "Now, based on the fact that I have just removed an illness that has left you a blithering vegetable for three years in order that we can have a nice, civilised chat, what are the odds I cannot make good on a threat?"

"This is a dream. Madness caused by the illness."

"You know it isn't. I can see into your mind," Dan said, matter of fact. "So the question is, do you want me to do that, Arthur? Do you want me to go to such *extremes* before you will talk to me?"

"No."

"That is good," Dan beamed. The smile appeared genuine. "This is progress. Now for the name."

"I..."

"Say it, Arthur."

"Dean."

"And who is Dean?"

"You know who..."

"I wish to hear it spill from *your* mouth, Arthur."

"Dean. My *son*."

"Your son," Dan echoed as he nodded an affirmation. "The son you've not seen for quite some time, by all accounts."

"A son who has abandoned his father in his hour of need. A son who has disowned me because I was simply too much trouble to cope with." Arthur was breathing heavily, and colour rose in his sallow cheek bones.

"Ah, this is good," Dan said clapping his hands together. "This is the stuff I came to hear!"

"Who the devil are you?"

"Oh, Arthur," Dan chuckled. "Will you please stop feeding me the lines?"

Arthur held his breath for a few moments. His eyes widened and he dropped his voice to a hush.

"Are you *him*?"

"Oh, no," Dan laughed. "But fret not, you will be meeting 'him' soon enough."

"But I don't understand," Arthur cried in terror. "Have I not been a pure soul?"

"In a word: *No*. In fact, your soul is quite grubby and will probably need a good *rinse* before I take it, you know, *downstairs*."

"You've come for my soul?" Arthur exclaimed. His eyes were wide with horror. "But you are not the devil. Who are you?"

"Well, I can see we're not going anywhere before we get this little hurdle out of the way," Dan grumbled. "My name is Ronove. And I'm a demon."

~

"A demon?"

"Now, please do not think any less of me," Dan said holding his hands up to ward off any recrimination. "If it helps, then I am actually a Marquis and Great Earl of Hell."

Arthur was dumbstruck. He simply stared at the creature masquerading as a man.

"Not impressed?" Dan sniffed. "Well, how about the fact that I command twenty legions of demons and have a way with words? Rhetoric, for example. Now surely you must be impressed by that. I did bring you back to the land of the listening, did I not? That must stand for something."

"I have gone mad. Here, in my last moments, sanity has left me," Arthur said to the ceiling.

"Not your last moments. Not quite," Dan assured him. "Not until my say so. Now, let's talk about Dean. Let's talk about your *relationship* with your son."

"I have no relationship. I have no son."

Dan eyed the old man impatiently. "I have to be a bit blunt here, Arthur. We're going to have a problem if you insist on going down this road. You're paralysed save for your vocal cords and I'm a demon with Hell at my disposal. How do you think this is going to go if you continue to piss me off?"

"All right, demon," Arthur conceded. "I had a son..."

"No, no, no," Dan said. "I need you to acknowledge you *have* a son, Arthur."

From nowhere a terrible growl filled the room and Arthur felt something on his face. A vile and pungent breeze almost scalded his skin, forcing him to squeeze his eyes shut as droplets of viscous fluid splattered his cheeks, some trickling into his mouth where his tongue was met with the taste of rancid meat. Arthur began to gag.

"Stop, stop!" he managed to utter between retches.

His eyes opened briefly to see something clinging to the ceiling, a beast that came with scales and teeth. Its mouth was agape, and its bulbous green tongue lolled like some awful snake searching for something to swallow and digest before shitting out the bones.

"Get it away from me!" he screamed.

"Remind me of your son's name, Arthur?" Dan commanded as he made a few notes on his clipboard.

"Dean! His name is Dean!"

The creature on the ceiling promptly vanished, taking the rancid taste with it.

"Thank Lucifer for that," Dan said with relief. "You wouldn't believe how much a monstrosity like *that* charges by the hour. Now, I have a question."

"What?" Arthur was weak with fear.

"Would you consider yourself to be a good father?"

"Yes." The response came through tight lips.

"And you base this on what, exactly?" Dan said after making a few more notes. The sound of the pen on the paper sounded like tiny screams behind a locked door.

"I was there for my son."

"Unlike *your* father?" Dan stated.

"My father worked all hours to support us," Arthur said in defiance. "He was a good man."

"Your father was a drunk who pissed away money that should have put food on the table," Dan replied, tapping the biro against his chin.

"When he wasn't at work, he was fucking whores. I like him. We talk often."

"You mock me."

"Not at all," Dan said with as much honesty a demon from Hades could muster. "But you fool yourself if you think being under the same roof as your child makes you a father."

"You know nothing about it, demon," Arthur spat.

"I know plenty," Dan countered. "But it seems you may need a prompt or two. Now, where to begin? Ah, I know! Remember this?"

Abruptly, Arthur was no longer supine and simpering in his bed. He was in the kitchen of his family home of sixty years. The kitchen was seventies kitsch, a place of Formica and red plastic. At the kitchen table, he saw himself aged thirty five, hunched over a sketchbook. The cartoon images were in bright, lurid colours.

Arthur found the ability to look upon the scene the way a member of the audience watches a play. He tried to establish a sense of order as he reached out to the nearest wall. The print on the paper consisted of a series of aqua green and gold circles that could have been applied by an errant child let loose with a *Spirograph* set. His fingers found the surface, but it yielded and shivered under his touch like jelly. He withdrew his hand, understanding that the image had little by way of physical substance.

There was a noise; the sound of footsteps running across the ceiling before they moved onto the stairs. The thumps became progressively louder and suddenly a small boy, no older than eight years of age, bounded into the room, a football held firmly in his hands.

Dean.

His son brushed a mop of dark hair out of his eyes. The image played out like a newsreel, as Arthur saw his younger self look up.

"I'll stop that right there," Dan said unexpectedly, and scene froze like a movie in *pause playback* mode. The demon was now standing beside Arthur.

"What are you doing?" Arthur asked.

"I need you to see something," Dan replied. He stepped up to the static image of young Arthur and pointed a finger at his frigid face.

"See that?"

"What?"

"The look of contempt on your brow," Dan explained. "It's plain for all."

"You're imagining such things to prove a point," Arthur said dismissively.

"A little harsh, if I may say?" Dan muttered. For a moment Arthur thought he could see the buds of tiny horns pushing against the skin of Dan's forehead.

"Have it your way, Arthur. Resume!"

The scene was alive again.

"Daddy, can we play football now?" Dean was asking. His voice was bright and hopeful.

"I told you, Daddy's busy, Dean," young Arthur said testily. "When I've finished this page I'll play football, okay?"

"But you said that an hour ago!" Dean stated throwing his head back in an exasperated fashion.

"You always seem to want to do something when I'm busy!" young Arthur snapped. "If you don't leave me in peace, I will not play with you at all."

"Pause that!"

Dan walked through the kitchen table and positioned himself between the two frozen images.

"What do you say to that, Arthur? Shunning and threatening a child because they're placing demands on you? Is that the action of a caring father?"

"Can you not see that I was working?" Arthur protested, but the way his eyes failed to connect with Dan's served his guilt up for all to see.

"*Doodles* are not work. They are merely an extension of the pipe dream you have carried with you throughout your life."

"Being a cartoonist was *not* a pipe dream," Arthur said. His face appeared hurt. "I was good, before the illness robbed me of my talent."

"Arthur, you're positively delusional," Dan giggled. "You were mediocre at best. Why not accept what you had? You made a fair bit of money from the estate agent business, right?"

"I wasn't put on this earth to be an estate agent," Arthur said. There wasn't any real conviction in his response. It was a small and frightened thing, as though intimidated by reality. "I always knew that. My passion was in drawing."

"Yes," Dan conceded briefly. "However, you can have all the passion in the world, but if you're shit then the odds of having a miserable existence start climbing the stairs, do they not?"

"I just needed a break, that's all." Arthur's tone was flat.

"Looking at the quality of those drawings, I'd say you had several breaks. All in the right arm. Let's move on, shall we?"

The kitchen winked out and Arthur found himself sitting in the back seat of a Triumph Herald he'd owned towards the end of the seventies. In the front seat, he could see the back of young Arthur's head. In the front passenger seat, Dean was chatting excitedly.

"Wasn't that a great film, Daddy?" he said making *whoosh* noises as he used his flattened out hands to mimic spaceships in flight.

"Yes, Dean," Arthur said impatiently. "Now don't keep going on about it."

Dean continued with his animated descriptions of his favourite parts of the film. Arthur could see the reflection of his other self in the rear view mirror. In almost slow motion he cast his eyes to the heavens.

"Hold it!" Dan again. "Got something written on your eyelids there, chief? Or is that dismissal I see?"

"I liked to concentrate when I was driving," Arthur shrugged. "Dean tended to distract me. It was a matter of safety."

"I think if you told a bigger lie, you'd end up with a tongue like mine!" Dan said. "Not dismissive, you say? Shall we continue?"

The scene resumed and saw Arthur reaching for the radio. He turned the dial until Dean was drowned out by the newscaster, who told them another series of power cuts were on the cards.

"Stop!"

Not Dan this time. Arthur was wiping at his eyes, the tears shockingly warm against his incorporeal cheeks.

"This is a skewed version of events."

"If you're seeing any shit on the carpet, remember that you're the one who's trampled it through the house," Dan sad bluntly. "It's time to move on."

In an instant the scene had changed again. The car was gone, replaced by a café, alive with the sounds of cutlery scraping against plates and the hiss of steam as coffee percolated behind the stainless steel counter.

Arthur and his son were sitting opposite each other, the remnants of a fried breakfast occupying the space on the table between them. Time had indeed moved on; several years, in fact. The mop-haired boy who had clutched footballs and made spaceships from his hands was now tall and athletic, with close-cropped dark hair and vivid blue eyes. He was wearing a University of Birmingham sweatshirt.

"You said you'd come and see the ceremony," Dean was saying. "I looked for you."

"I was busy," Arthur heard his younger self say. "I can't just drop work. I have a business to run. Besides, your mother was there to see you get your award."

"I wanted *you* there, Dad," Dean said. Current Arthur could see the how his son's eyes were cold, and the muscles in his cheeks twitched with supressed anger. "I *needed* to see you there."

"Why on Earth was it so important?" Arthur was taking a sip of his tea and looking out of the window to the street where people walked by.

"I don't know, Dad. It was my *graduation*. You tell me?"

"Aaaaand, freeze frame!" Dan interjected. "But you couldn't tell him could you, Arthur? How would any father be able to do such a thing as admit they begrudged the success of their own child?"

"That's nonsense!" Arthur protested.

"*Truth hurts more than a hot poker up the anus* as my boss often says," Dan stated. "Admit it, Arthur, your son is gifted. He graduated with honours in graphic design and within three weeks had an apprenticeship with *Dark Horse Comics*. He'd stolen your dream. As far as you were concerned, he'd snatched the golden goose and all you got was a big, fat bag of sour grapes. You pushed him away. He didn't want that but it's the only thing you offered."

"His mother was the one who maintained the family. She kept it all together."

"This would be Sally, right?" Dan said. "The woman who fucked off as soon as Dean left home because you were a self-satisfied bore who left her unfulfilled for years?"

"She said we'd grown apart," Arthur muttered. His heart was soured by the memory. "She just wanted to be happy."

"Well, she was happy for quite some time," Dan stated. "After your divorce she shacked up with the guy she'd been having an affair with for the last three years of your marriage. They fucked so often it was a wonder she was able to walk in a straight line. She died a happy soul. Well, as I say to the boss, *ya can't win 'em all*, right?"

"You're a monster who enjoys tormenting the weak," Arthur growled.

"And your point is?"

"I was a good," Arthur began, but Dan rode roughshod over him,

"Not good. Bad. Very bad. Jeez you are one stubborn mule," Dan said scratching his head wearily. "And don't get me wrong here. I like bad. It keeps me in a job after all. But you're blaming your son for your own actions. Frankly, that's very naughty. He thinks that you don't love him, have never loved him. Looking at the footage, I can see he has a point."

"Stop, Demon. Please." Tears were back.

"He's married now. Did you know that?"

"No."

"Yes. To a wonderful woman. Wendy," Dan explained. "She works at his studio. She's a witch, of course. *Witch Wendy*, it has a ring to it, don't you think? But the soppy hag loves your son so much. She knows Dean is not in a good place. Every night he tries to find resolution in a bottle of wine. Something has contributed to a severe lack of self-esteem, it seems. My money is on having a shitty father."

Arthur remained quiet. Dan continued regardless.

"Well, Wendy may be a daughter of Satan, but she'll do anything for your son. She summoned me, though he's not *in the know* on this, so to speak. And let's face it, since she's given up her soul for the cause, and I was swinging by anyway, it seemed churlish not to do her a favour."

"Favour?"

"Now we get to the point of it all, dear Arthur," Dan said in a dramatic tone. "You need to sort out this *will* business. I mean, leaving all your estate to a dog's home, for Satan's sake? What were you thinking?"

"I was angry," Arthur sighed. "I thought Dean had abandoned me."

"And now?"

Arthur sighed. "I concede that this burden is mine."

Dan watched the figure in the bed seem to shrink as Arthur made reality's acquaintance. The old man sobbed, but it was a quiet affair, punctuated by small gasps for air.

"I'm not looking for atonement here, Arthur," Dan whispered. "I'm looking for action. Besides,

Dean's wily witch has done a little jiggery-pokery and placed a curse on every dog that benefits from your will. Something to do with spontaneously turning inside out, I forget the details."

"What do I do to fix things?" Arthur asked. His Adam's apple pumped away snot that had trickled into the back of his throat.

"Look at this," Dan said turning the clip board around so that Arthur could see it.

"What is it?" Arthur asked with a sniff.

"This is your new will. It states that you intend to hand your estate to Dean, the rightful heir. Dean needs to know you care about him. This little thing will help him feel good about himself. And make Wendy a happy hag. Everyone wins."

"How is that possible? I signed it five years ago. In law, I no longer have mental capacity to amend it."

"Just sign it, Arthur, and let me sweat through the peripheral stuff."

Arthur could suddenly feel the weight pinning his right arm to the bed begin to recede. He wiggled his fingers, relishing the sensation of the coarse duvet under his touch. It had been a long time since sense and reasoning had found such unity. His illness had robbed him of so much, and this sliver of normalcy was his window on what once was.

"Take the pen," Dan ordered.

Arthur took the biro from him.

"X marks the spot," Dan brought the sheets of paper into view. They were white and fresh and headed with the phrase, *Last Will and Testament of Arthur Dean Conlon*.

"The sheets appear new," Arthur observed. "They will know it's fake."

"My, you are such a worrier!" Dan said with a grin. He nodded as Arthur signed the sheets. "That's the ticket."

Dan retrieved the sheets of paper, and Arthur's ability to move his arm ended and it flopped onto the bed, one finger outstretched as though pointing to all things lost. Holding the papers in front of him, Dan whispered incomprehensible words, and Arthur watched, amazed, as the white sheets became withered and creased, as though age had suddenly caught up with them.

"There." Dan admired his handiwork. "As good as – oh, whatever, you get the gist."

"Now what?" Arthur asked, dejected.

"Well, I guess we've done what has been asked of us and we return to the natural order of things."

"Am I destined for Hell?" Arthur enquired. A shudder ran through him.

"Did you really have to ask that?" Dan said with a wink. "Don't be too concerned. You get used to the heat after a while."

"How long do I have left on this Earth?"

"Well, if I was to say part of my scope is harvesting old souls who are not long for this world, does that give you a hint?" Dan said this as though it would be of help.

"When will it hap—"

Dan's arm snaked out and punched a hole into the old man's side. The fist passed through the ribs and the lungs and into the heart.

The fingers extended and Dan had a good root around.

"Where are you?" he giggled. "Ah, gotcha, you little bugger."

He dragged his hand from the ragged hole left in Arthur Conlon's inert body. In his grip was a bloodied, writhing mass of flesh and veins. A small cavity opened up and gave forth a scream that reverberated about him. The forked tongue darted out from Dan's mouth and licked the bloodied shape in his hands. The demon's body shivered as he relished the taste. A new soul was a delicacy he just could not resist.

"Yummy," his eyes closed. "Guilt has a flavour all of its own."

The tiny mouth let go another thin screech.

"Hush now, Arthur," Dan cradled the ravaged soul to him. "Let's just keep you nice and warm for a while."

Dan pressed the embryo into his body, where it was first absorbed by the folds of his garments, then by the layers of fatty tissue beneath until no longer visible. He could feel it, of course, writhing under his skin in consummate torment.

"Well, not strictly *warm* in the usual context. But you know what I mean."

His work done, Demon Dan closed the bubble and time resumed. In the bed, Arthur appeared at peace, but the soul rummaging around the demon's guts suggested a new reality.

"Has he gone?" Amanda was standing in the doorway. She had a mug of coffee in her hands.

"Yes," he confirmed. "It was peaceful."

"I shall ring his son," she said sadly. "He asked to be notified straight away. It seems unjust, doesn't it?"

Dan was intrigued by her sentiment. "How so, dear Amanda?"

"He visits every weekend and on the very day he can't make it, his father slips away," she explained sadly.

"Yes. What *were* the odds?"

"Will you stay with Arthur for a moment?" Amanda said as she passed him his coffee. "While I make the call?"

"Of course," Dan replied taking the coffee from her. "I felt that, at the end, Arthur and I became quite *close.*"

"Careful," Amanda cautioned as she nodded towards the mug. "It's hotter than a thousand devils."

"Thank you," he said. "You're an..."

"Angel?" she offered with a grin.

"I do hope not," he said.

"Oh, you *are* naughty, Daniel," her lashes bobbing. She left the room, but her coy giggles followed her out.

Dan looked at the coffee as tendrils of steam made swirls in the air. And then he drank it in three gulps.

"She makes damned good coffee," he whispered to the room. "Shame she's destined for *other* places. Unlike you, dear fellow." He patted his belly where Arthur's blistering soul responded with tiny kicks.

"Ah," Dan picked up the will. "Almost forgot about you."

He pulled open a drawer in the bedside cupboard and placed the aged sheets inside. Amanda and her colleagues would find them as they readied the room for another corpse-in-waiting.

Then, with one last glance towards the human shell lying on the bed, Demon Dan winked out of this world and made his way back to his own. Through ethereal planes separating one dimension from the next, his transcendental journey was guided by the insistent shrieks and cries of the Damned.

And out of all those lost, no one screamed louder than Arthur Dean Conlon.

Disturbia

Through the window of his prison, Mark Winters watched the quiet, empty street. Fear churned his guts like a bad dinner, his forehead, a corrugated landscape of pale white flesh, pressed up against the cool glass pane.

Trembling hands clutched at the curtains, as though letting go of the flimsy material would have him spinning from the face of the Earth. Breaths came as long, controlled sighs, a way of regulating the physical effects of his malady. It was learned behaviour, a product of *the bulletins*.

Beyond the glass, his little slice of home may have appeared sedate, but it was the jittering lid of a simmering saucepan. The dangers were there, hiding in plain sight. His body an unstable entity because of it, his face bore the scars of the physiological effects of chronic anxiety, the corners of his mouth trembled as though he were on the brink of tears, every few seconds his right eye would spasm like the furtive wink of a poor liar.

Across the road there were three large, detached houses, each with beige double garages and bay windows of dark plastic frames and leaded glass. In front of each house, an expanse of lawn that, three months ago, would have been tennis-court smooth. A quiet, pristine piece of suburbia, a million miles away from the chaos of earning a living.

But the lawns were no longer neat. They were uneven rectangles of tall grass, the blades undulating at the touch of the late summer breeze, the movement creating a soft lilting hiss, like the sound of...

Snakes, his mind said. *Lying in those blades of grass, waiting to slither up to your house, through the letterbox, writhing into the hall and then in here, and their mouths will be wide and the fangs will be wet with venom, and they will bite you, pump you full of poison until your tongue swells and turns purple and clogs your throat, and as you choke on it they will all watch you die with those unfeeling, black eyes.*

Winters stumbled away from the window, his skin a greasy sheen of sweat. He fell onto the sofa, the dark leather squeaking as he landed. He grabbed a cushion – a furry green thing that had always reminded him of an 80s fairground *Gonk* – and clasped it to his chest as would a child watching a scary TV show. His breathing was ragged, his head becoming light, and his vision blurred as he began to hyperventilate.

In the depths of his mind *the bulletin* came to him. It was now becoming a reflex, as natural as the ever-present state of fear.

"To avoid a panic attack you must follow three simple rules: Rule one – you must breathe in through your nose; this will fill up your lower lungs and then your upper lungs. Rule two – you must hold your breath for the count of three. Say this in your head, not out loud. Rule three – exhale very slowly through your mouth, purse your lips as though you are stoking a fire. As you do so, relax the muscles in your face, jaw, shoulders, and stomach. You must repeat this several times until you are in control."

And so it was that practice kicked in and Winters fought off his latest anxiety attack, following the instructions to the letter. As his mind returned to whatever constituted normality these days, he became aware he was sitting in a pool of his own urine.

He stood and headed for the kitchen to find something to clear up the mess. There was no shame, only relief.

Last time he wet himself, he'd been in bed.

~

When Winters had first experienced what was now described by *the bulletins* as 'The Great Fear', he had been in a shopping centre looking for a Christmas card and gift for Rachel, his wife of 30 years. The gift was meant to be token; their real present to each other was reservations to see out the New Year skiing in Aspen. It was one of the many passions they had shared; their thirst for travel was another.

It wasn't hard to recall the events of that terrible evening. Hyper-vigilance was an effective means of recall. Only the bad stuff, of course, only the stuff that perpetuated *the fear*.

But it was *love* that drew him to the glitter and glass of the Bull Ring Centre in Birmingham. Before marriage, he and Rachel had gone to the same school – St Michael's Church of England Comprehensive – and the same night spots – notably *Faces French* on Hagley Road. The school had been bulldozed to pave the way for a housing estate. The nightclub had been refashioned into a fast food restaurant. They often joked their relationship had outlived the very things that had brought them together.

No joking these days. Rachel was dead, her body stowed in the chest freezer in the garage.

The thought should have weighed heavy on him but instead it was as though he were thinking about a distant memory of little relevance. The Great Fear had a habit of pulling a curtain down on the pain, his worldview had no place, the overwhelming power of self-obsession – *self-preservation* – weakened objectivity. There was no such thing as grief or anger, emotion was subservient to the master that was fear. And under its yolk, everything stooped at its passing.

The shopping centre had been pretty quiet, most Christmas shoppers having taken advantage of the flexibility afforded by late night trade. Winters had been no different, he'd waited with the patience retirement afforded. Selling his financial consultancy firm three years ago and reaping the rewards ever since, he was no longer a slave to fiscal risk assessments and insurance liability schemes.

Any benefits belonged to him and his wonderful wife.

He'd been on the main escalators, thinking about their pending trip, when the pervading sense of unease came upon him, unexpectantly.

As it took hold, Winters had gripped the rail, the plastic squeaking beneath his palm. He could now recall the faces of those who were around him. An older woman who was ahead began to teeter on her legs, and a small whimper came from her as she looked about her, fretful and confused.

The escalator climbed and the head of a large, aged security guard came into view, like a new sunrise on the horizon. But the man fell to his knees, his face screwed up as though in agony, and Winters had been able to see the tears flowing from eyes that had been clamped shut. Then the guard curled up in a foetal position and put a thumb in his mouth before calling out for his mother.

All about him, the screams came, terrified and frantic and, in the way forest animals would stampede ahead of an unexpected danger, people ran. It didn't matter if others were in the way, or if they were on escalators, or in shops, the movement was chaotic; elderly men and women fleeing for their lives, some going down and succumbing to the feet of those not inclined to avoid them, the sharp snap of bones, the squelch of organs popping under the onslaught.

Winters had been with them, fighting his way back down the escalator, his hands lashing out at those who were not quick enough, there was nothing that could have stopped him getting away from the cause of the terror. It was feral and wanton, beyond reason.

He'd managed to get outside, and that was when he saw that the whole city was scattered, the populous screaming and weeping, running from a danger of which no one appeared to have any knowledge or understanding.

That was to come later.

When the bulletins began.

~

Winters had no memory of how he'd fought his way from the city centre and back to his house. He recalled the terror, the absolute desperation to get home, where he knew that he'd be safe.

There was no explaining the certainty of such a nuance, but it was powerful, as though the thought of home was a temporary antidote for his fear.

He'd found Rachel lying in a heap in the hall. Her mousey hair, long and flecked with grey, was a tangled mane beneath her. Her face had been a horrible blue colour, glassy eyes staring up at the ceiling, but her body was face down, one of her legs bent into a zigzag and resting on the last few steps of the staircase, a length of sparkling Christmas garland coiled about her ankle. The stairway was partially decorated with fairy lights and thick tinsel boas, the traditional beginnings of Yuletide in the Winters' abode.

Winters had collapsed in the hallway; his beloved Rachel was gone but the fear inside him was not. He had quietly wept, but he even back then he'd realised that anxiety was the mother of narcissism. His grief was eaten by the omnipotent terror still sending tremulous waves through his body.

Impassive, he'd stayed with Rachel, stroking her hair, his eyes avoiding her dead gaze by focusing on a box of baubles waiting to go on the tree they'd ordered from the local garden centre only a few days before.

The tree never came.

~

After cleaning up the puddle of urine on his sofa, Winters took a shower, allowing the hot water to cleanse his body, the heat soothing his beleaguered spirit.

The shower gel became foam, thick, fat wads slapping into the tray, each perfumed detonation making him shiver, his startle response in its usual state of overdrive. There had been no real information as to what was happening in the world outside. Frustration was easily overpowered by the relentless terror, the need to be safe sacrosanct in these awful times.

The bulletins came four times a day, sequential episodes on the TV, black screen, white words, and an automated calm yet authoritative male voice that cited advice – the method for averting a panic attack, for example – or a reminder to stay in doors to avoid 'the threat'.

As to the exact nature of said 'threat', this remained esoteric, perhaps the greatest mystery to befall the Earth since the demise of the dinosaur. The mere thought of what lurked in the quiet *cul de sac* beyond his front door had him shuddering. The world had changed in such a short space of time. Perhaps not the world itself, but his *access* to it.

'It's a small world' was an adage bandied around all too often, and now it was getting smaller with the advent of the Internet. This was one aspect where things *were* different. The access to any form of media was down, limited only to *the bulletin*. Other than this the utilities – electricity, water and gas – remained operational. At least somewhere things appeared to be business as usual.

In the few months leading up to the current state of play there was only the election to consider: two mainstay parties, arguing on their version of a better world. There were some similarities in policy, if not politic; a unilateral acknowledgement people were living longer, and the social care system could no longer sustain those in their seasoned years.

Debates and sound bites counted for nothing in the end.

No one seemed to have any answers.

~

In the few days after finding his beloved Rachel at the foot of the stairs, the deliveries came. Left on the doorstep, the large cardboard box had the words 'Emergency Rations' stencilled in bright red letters. *The bulletins* made clear these provisions would be expected to last seven days. Replacements would arrive each week. And they had indeed done so, for more days than Winters could remember.

Many things came to mind as he'd opened the box on that first day, pulling cans and dried goods from the carton and arranging them in lines on the kitchen counter. But dominating all the ambiguities was a suspicion that what he (and his neighbours for that matter) experienced was distilled down to one word.

Quarantine.

The anxiety such a word evoked ensured his mind erased the implications of such an edict almost immediately. His head had felt suddenly light, and he'd slapped his hands on the counter to stabilise himself, his breathing rapid and shallow, the ideal climate to deoxygenate his blood. This was at a time when the advice from the bulletins was scant.

He'd ridden it out, pressing his face to the counter, the cool marble welcome against his cheek. The need to blink his eyes a hundred times, overpowering. By the time he had counted to one hundred, the word 'quarantine' had been forgotten.

~

The relief parcels came at some point in the early hours of Monday mornings, when he was asleep.

Sleep was a strange affair, perpetual anxiety created an indescribable level of fatigue. When Winters climbed into bed, rather than fear the possibilities of being left defenceless ramping up the terror, he found he would merely wink out. And the blackness would be total. Fatigue would come in waves at ten in the evening, slumber claiming him by ten fifteen. At nine in the morning his eyes would flick open.

Every day, without fail.

And when he woke, his first thought was not images of a lingering dream but sounds, the gentle rustling, the beating of tiny wings, and the shrill calls of birdsong. In those delicate sounds, he found a residue of comfort and peace, an acceptance of sorts of all that was going on, even though he had no idea what it actually meant.

Then these emotions would be swept away by the ferocious sense of foreboding, and the world became a place where the sinister and deadly lurked outside his front door, a place from which his only protection were the walls of his home, *the bulletin*, and the weekly food drop.

With great ease, these things became all he needed in the world.

~

Winters had several rituals.

When he entered the kitchen, he avoided the black tiles on the chequered floor. Before going into the lounge, he had to tap the door jamb ten times, but only on the spot where there was a small blister in the cream paintwork. Prior to opening the door to collect his weekly parcel, he had to wash his hands in warm water for forty-seconds, and again after he had brought the parcel into the house. He could not explain it, but each compulsion seemed to blunt the foreboding enough for him to continue with his day, and the moments were measured by these rituals, the ceaseless countdown of a dreadful timepiece.

Adding to the ever present routine was the truck.

The truck had a similar timetable to *the bulletins*. A great, grey beast with black windows and high, featureless side panels. The vehicle had first appeared on the third day of Winters' neurosis-fuelled exile, announced by the rumbling growl of its engine as it stalked the quiet streets. At first that great engine sounded like thunder rolling across the sky, adding to Winters' ever present sense of doom.

Then the truck pulled into the close and followed the kerb, turning three-sixty, its huge cab pointing at the exit when it stopped with a thick squeak of chunky breaks.

The grey behemoth would sit there for ten minutes, the engine grumbling as it idled. Then it would leave. This happened twice a day – at 10am and 5pm – and always for a duration of 10 minutes, no more, no less.

Winters may have had questions about the purpose of the truck, and what it was waiting for every day, but when he thought about it too much his anxiety blunted his concern, and he quickly became disinterested.

After a week of visits, the arrival of the truck was as much a part of his daily routine as going to bed and waking up the next day.

But as he stepped out of the shower and towelled off, his mandate for equilibrium did something quite unexpected.

It changed without warning.

~

There was irony in that the change began with normalcy.

He woke up.

He showered.

He made breakfast, had two mugs of black, decaf coffee, all this time listening to *the bulletin* and its banal rhetoric.

He heard the truck, the brass letterbox on the front door stuttering as the vehicle turned into the close and parked, the familiar grumble of the engine ever-present.

There came another sound, and its unfamiliar nature had Winters engaging in his proactive breathing exercises. A door was opening, the clatter and clunk of locks being thrown, the ensuing creak of hinges.

Then the voices came.

The chatter was excitable and hurried; the pace, staccato; the footfalls, heavy, with no hint of hesitation; a stark contrast to the leaden steps Winters took on legs where muscles were cramping with tension. He avoided the black tiles and tapped the door jamb the pre-requisite number of times. He got to the lounge window, his mind screaming at him, the madness of it, *run away, hide, damn you, this is not for you.*

But his rituals provided a buffer, keeping such warnings at bay, at least for the time being. He peered out from behind the curtains, his face a mask frozen by trepidation, the muscles in his right eye going into spasm, making the scene beyond the glass appear as though he was watching sleazy 35mm movies on an archaic projector.

He recognised the people straight away.

Mr and Mrs Morley were both in their seventies. Joe Morley was a retired head teacher, his wife, Christine, a librarian. Joe was still a tall, proud man with a bald crown and hair usually clipped neatly over his ears.

It was no surprise to Winters to see Joe's hair was longer than usual, and his locks danced in the breeze as white gossamer threads.

These days Christine was only slightly shorter than her husband, and only because her shoulders were stooped with age. Both of the Morleys were smiling, their faces showing no sign of fear. Instead there was something akin to excitement.

Joe was pointing enthusiastically at the roof of the truck which sat there, impassive, its windows as black as a starless night.

Winters thought about opening the window. Something told him he would only be safe if he traced a figure of eight ten times on the sill. He did this and gently eased open the pane.

Joe's voice came to him. "Oh, my, Chrissy," he said in awe as his right hand lifted, an extended index finger pointed at the roof of the truck. "Look at them. Aren't they just beautiful?"

Christine clapped her hands together like a child receiving a birthday gift. "Oh, and their beautiful song. Have you ever heard such a sound, Joe?"

The Morleys moved towards the truck, eyes looking at the roof. At their approach the back doors clunked and eased open. Winters watched as the couple climbed into the vehicle without hint of hesitation. The doors closed and, after a pause, the truck drove off, leaving Winters' confused gaze to follow its passage until it disappeared from view.

~

The day after the Morleys climbed into the back of the truck, Winters saw the corpse.

The thought of his neighbours took him back to his lounge window (after the tapping of the door-jamb ritual, of course).

He found himself troubled with questions. Why had Joe and Christine left their house, and how had they been able to do so? What were they looking at on the roof of the truck? Where were they now? All these notions rattled in his head as he scanned the Morleys house for signs of life.

Instead, he found only death – in the upstairs window of the house next door to the Morley property.

The body belonged to an elderly man called Arthur Stokes, a friend who Winters had known for over eight years. Arthur was an avid gardener and the allotment he tended at the back of his house was a source of fascinating discussion over a beer or two on Arthur's patio.

Arthur was a jolly man; a smile, and a quip always on his lips. No smile now though. Just a gaping hole as his pale, dead face pressed against the glass of his bedroom window, gravity dragging the head downwards as the face remained stuck to the glass, reminding Winters of Edvard Munch's expressionist painting *The Scream*.

Engaging his breathing exercises, Winters stepped away – not only from the terrible sight across the street, but from a brief flash of memory: the image of Rachel, her blue face framed in packs of ice as he lowered her gently into the chest freezer, closing the lid as anxiety smothered his grief.

And so it was that the fleeting memory of great loss was swallowed by The Great Fear. Rachel in the freezer, Arthur and his endless scream at his bedroom window, forever prisoners behind a wall of terror.

~

The woods are still, the only sound are footfalls as Winters' boots step upon the bracken, the snaps and crunches reminding him of breakfast cereals doused in milk, the start of a new dawn, a new day.

Someone should write a song about it he thinks, and smiles at his own trite joke.

Another noise comes to him, and at once he is filled with an overwhelming sense of peace. The fluttering of wings is back, a light, deft symphony drifting across the dreamscape, making the sounds of his clumsy progress through the woodland seem hapless and maladroit. He turns his head, seeking out the source of this striking aural entity. He happens upon its creators soon enough.

Four blackbirds are sitting on the haphazard carcass of a fallen tree trunk. Their heads bob in time with their song, and each note feels it is penetrating his soul, creating a feeling – a concord – he has not known before; his mind and his heart embrace it, relishing it as one would the embrace of a loved one.

The refrain continues, the shrill chirps now make Winters seem not part of the world at all, but only a passenger, a tourist passing through on his way to another land, another adventure.

He becomes lost in the shrill melody and something inside of him yearns to be free of his corporeal form, and as he taps into this feeling, so he awakes and finds, to his complete and utter joy, the rapture is not doused by consciousness, and like the incredible sentiment of his seemingly endless delight, something else has followed him from his dreamscape and into the physical world.

The dizzying song of four blackbirds.

~

Winters sat up in bed, birdsong in his head, and a great euphoria in his heart.

There was no fear, the concept of such a thing now as distant to him as Betelgeuse. He swung his legs out of bed, pushed his feet into his slippers, and made his way across the bedroom where his blue-towelled dressing gown was draped over the back of a chair.

After putting on his robe he made his way downstairs, and the lilting sound of the blackbirds was now a soundtrack for his journey through the house. He made breakfast. Had a cup of coffee, poured a second cup, and walked freely out of the kitchen and into the lounge, the door jamb shunned for the first time in months.

As usual the TV was on, but there was no bulletin. The white words and black background were replaced with the four blackbirds, sitting on their fallen tree trunk, and the cadence of shrill chirps now deputised for the automated announcer.

Winters leaned towards the images, hands reaching out, fingers splayed. "You're so beautiful. I want to be with you. I want to be free."

Another sound came to him as his fingertips touched the screen.

The truck.

A dark shadow crossed the lounge, momentarily muting the light as though a cloud had passed before the sun, and the thunder of the vehicle as it lumbered into the close to execute its turn added to the impression that a great storm was about to hit.

There was no foreboding; quite the opposite, in fact. Winters was having to fight against great euphoric waves, the truck was no longer a mystery to him, it was his ride to freedom, he knew this with a certainty that was as dizzying as it was beyond reproach.

His feet took him to the front door, and when he threw it open, he saw two things that made him dizzy with delight.

First, the truck had pulled up outside his path and now waited patiently, its engine growling like a sleeping tiger. The windows of the cab were black and impenetrable. Winters giggled and waved all the same.

Secondly, he saw the birds. There were four of them of course, and they hopped and bobbed on the roof of the truck, their song strident and exquisite. They hopped to the back of the truck and, as they neared the edge, the two rear doors opened slowly, deliberately.

Without hesitation Winters walked down the path, his steps light as though his elation were physically lifting him from the tangle of weeds and grass threatening to ensnare him. He went to the rear of the truck, his eyes never leaving the birds as they peered down at him with their beaded black eyes, their yellow beaks sending out their endless, beautiful refrain.

Winters climbed into the truck and sat down on the bench running the length of the interior. Opposite him was a lifeless, widescreen monitor. However, as the doors closed, the monitor came to life and the blackbirds were back in all their glory, the image throwing watery light all about him.

"Oh my," Winters whispered, the smile on his lips so insistent it made his cheeks ache. As the birds frolicked on screen, white letters appeared at their feet.

It is time. Are you ready to go?

Winters' smile faltered for a moment. "I'm not sure. This is my home. My Rachel is here."

The images of the blackbirds faded, and the bulletin returned: black screen, white letters.

Do you wish to stay?

And not only did the bulletin return, so did The Great Fear, the crippling anxiety that had choked the world.

His body shuddered, muscles pulling into great, shivering spasms as adrenalin flowed wanton and unchecked, sending his central nervous system into meltdown.

"Yes!" he screamed. "Yes, I am ready to go."

No sooner had he said these words than the birds came back to the screen, their wonderful image spangled as tears misted his eyes. As though a switch was thrown, all anxiety left him, and his sigh of relief was long, the sound of a user getting a long-needed fix.

Winters sat back, the vibration of the engine throbbing through the hard wooden bench, but the comfort it brought to him was beyond description.

With the birds on the monitor cavorting under his rapturous gaze, Winters felt the truck move off, birdsong now keeping him company for however long his journey was to last.

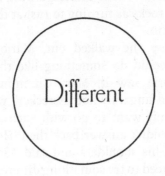

Different

Henry Potts adjusted his tie. It was salmon pink, the knot expertly tied into the broad wedge of a full Windsor. *No half measures today*, he thought. *Everything is to be just so.*

Nothing could spoil the moment. It was a special day: Halloween, his *favorite* night of the year, and to top it all, *Marjorie was coming home.*

It had been nine months since his wife had left their detached house in quiet, leafy Norwich. Their sedate, well-kept life came as part of the spoils of hard work. Henry was a managing director of a local supermarket chain, and his wife owned a florist's shop in the town center.

However, their thirty-four-year marriage had been in the doldrums for at least half of that time. There was a sense of inevitability when the affair came, confirmation that a roving eye and a sexless marriage are not conducive to ongoing fidelity. When Marjorie found Henry in the marital bed with Mary Cummings, his young PA, it merely confirmed what the Potts' already knew – their marriage wasn't so much as on the rocks as turning to rust at the bottom of the ocean.

The day she walked out, Marjorie asked why he would do something like this to her. As Marjorie saw it, Mary Cummings was a 'brash and ungainly homewrecker', why would he suddenly want to go with such a woman? Henry couldn't answer back then. He'd merely shrugged his shoulders and said, "Sometimes, you just need to try something different."

On hearing this, Marjorie's round and ample face had crumpled into despair. "You never gave me an opportunity to be anything other than the same," she said, and left the house with a barely stifled sob.

The irony lay in that Henry didn't really know how much of his life Marjorie filled until she was no longer a part of it. None of this came to light more so than at dinner, where he would set two places at the dining table, Marjorie's favorite dinner service – Denby Regency, sixteen-piece with a teal trim – laid out in all its majesty, as he toyed with his take-away or microwave meal, appetite dissolving like an exorcised spirit.

For the first few months of their separation, he had only set the table for one, and engaged in all the activities he'd traditionally not been able to do at dinner, such as reading books and watching *Bargain Hunt* on his iPad. Yet as he did such things, reclaiming some of his pre-marital identity, he would see something or read something that would have him looking up with a comment on his lips, only to remember times had changed, and his only companion was his ever-increasing sense of guilt.

Another ambiguity with Marjorie's departure was his total loss of interest in Mary Cummings, or any other woman for that matter. At fifty-three, Henry's physique was kept trim by his daily three-mile run, and while his short hair was what salons these days called 'Arctic Blonde,' his face remained boyish in features if not veneer. As the months without Marjorie passed by, his penchant for vanity became an early casualty; his libido curled up and died soon after.

He'd been in a fugue for quite a while, but as of now, things were different, things were about to change back to how they once were. Tonight, there would be laughter in the house again – Marjorie would be there, and they would talk and resolve their differences, as he expunged his guilt, making way for a new beginning for them both.

Vibrant and light, Henry's heart beat out an accord against his chest. The feeling was made manifest by a beaming smile that came back to him from the bedroom mirror. Admiring his handiwork made it easier to ignore the chaos of the bedroom behind him. The duvet was heaped upon the king-sized mattress, a gray, grimy mountain of duck and down. Beside the bed, plates and bowls were smeared with dried food, and the beige carpet was littered with crumbs and hairballs.

Henry walked across the bedroom, trampling upon clothing strewn across the floor, and up to a pair of brown suede moccasins that were parked beneath Marjorie's long-abandoned dressing table, where a small wicker chair provided them with shelter. He went to the chair and pulled it to one side before stepping into the shoes, sighing at the feel of the soft material against his bare feet.

After taking his suit jacket from the back of the bedroom door, he pulled it on, buttoning it up and ignoring just how loose a fit it had become.

~

In the kitchen, Henry watched the pots and pans bubbling on the hob. He could not wait for his wife to see how organised he'd become in the kitchen. This had been her domain after all. She was a fine cook, and expert baker. At one point she was thinking of auditioning for *The Great British Bake Off*, but she'd not gone through with the application.

Her confidence was a fragile thing. She'd loved the home, she'd loved homemaking, and it had come as a surprise to Henry that his wife had made no attempt to reclaim her home since she'd left. It was as though she just did not want to return here, the memories perhaps too painful.

Like most of her prize possessions, the stove was olive green. *The color of her eyes*, he thought fondly. Carrots and Maris Piper potatoes simmered away, the lids of the pans jittering and giving out steam. A larger pan was par-boiling King Edward potatoes for roasting later. To the left of the stainless-steel sink unit, a steamer took care of florets of cauliflower and broccoli; the surface of stacked plastic trays were a shroud of condensation, turning the vegetables inside to vague silhouettes.

Henry had everything planned to the letter. Once the vegetables were *al dente*, he would store them ready for re-heat later. The centerpiece – a leg of Welsh lamb – would go into the oven to slow roast at four o'clock, ready to serve at nine. Then Henry would prepare the house for Halloween festivities, hanging up the streamers and garlands, carving the pumpkins and putting them out onto the porch. No kids ever came, but that didn't matter, it was all part of the fun, part of the *ritual*.

Marjorie was set to arrive at 6:30, when it was sure to be dark.

Over the sink unit, a window provided a view of their quiet cul-de-sac. The houses were all detached, each with a double garage, suburban uniformity alive and kicking. Smiling, he looked out as he washed-up the sieve in the sink; some of his neighbors already had their jack-o'-lanterns in their windows.

He'd loved Halloween since he was a boy, the spectacle of it, the thrill of scary movies and stories. His parents were advocates, and it was only natural that Henry was to continue with the tradition, even though he and Marjorie couldn't have children. They'd tried, of course, but conception just never happened. Henry felt a pang of guilt and poured himself a glass of single malt to put errant shame to sleep.

He walked about the kitchen, prodding vegetables with a fork so that they weren't overdone. On his way to the fridge to get cream and butter for mashing the Maris Pipers potatoes, Henry cast a furtive glance at the block of money on the breakfast bar.

There was more than five thousand pounds in ten and twenty-pound notes. The stack was bound together by a thick, blue elastic band he'd retrieved from a ledger in the attic. The fit was tight, bowing the cash in the middle. As he passed by, he patted the money.

Salvation costs, he thought before carrying on with his cooking.

~

The doorbell rang out at 6:30 sharp. Henry was in the process of positioning the last of the silverware on the rosewood dining table. He checked over the layout, nodded, and let go a long sigh. He removed the apron he'd been wearing to keep his suit clean and headed for the front door, stopping only to smooth out his hair in the hallway mirror. The doorbell rang again, this time for longer as impatience appeared to kick in.

His moccasins squeaked on the parquet floor as he hurried to the door where two shapes could be seen through the *faux* stained-glass panel. "I'm coming! I'm coming!" he said as he undid the locks and yanked on the handle.

The two men standing on the coir 'Welcome' mat shuffled on the spot. The first man was big, at least six-four in height, and his belly hung low in his gray coveralls. He wore a matching baseball cap with a GRAVES, INC. patch stitched onto it. On his breast pocket, a name badge told Henry the man's name was HARDY.

His partner was much smaller, but he was lean, and his hazel eyes were shrewd and glinted in the porch lights. His name badge said LAUREL and he referred to a silver clipboard in his hands. He rifled the pages and clucked his tongue as he skimmed the sheets.

"Got a delivery for a Mr. Henry Potts?"

"Yes, I am he." Henry nodded and gave them both a big smile, which neither of them returned.

Laurel spoke as he adjusted the strap of a small brown satchel that hung off his shoulder. "You got the money?"

"Yes. It's inside."

Laurel looked at Henry, his thin lips twitching as though he was about to have a stroke. "This is the part where you give us the money."

Henry frowned and crossed his arms. It was a trait he'd adopted from his father and had served him well in the retail trade. When he spoke, his voice was firm and authoritative.

"Well, I think I'd prefer to see my wife first."

This time it was Hardy who spoke, and his voice had as much presence as his physique. "Give us the money or she stays in the van."

Henry looked beyond the two men. At the bottom of the drive, a dark Ford Transit was parked up on the curb, obscuring their interactions from anyone across the road.

"What's it to be?" Hardy said. "You paying us now, or is she going back?"

Henry could see there was no further negotiation on offer. "Wait here." He headed off to the kitchen and returned with the block of notes.

Laurel held out his hand. "I'll have that, thank you." He took the money and stowed it in his satchel. "Right. We'll go and get her."

"Can you escort her to the dining room?" Henry said.

Hardy scowled. "We deliver to the house. *Fitting* is extra."

Henry sighed. "Will you accept a debit card?"

~

Marjorie killed herself on what would have been their 35th wedding anniversary. By that time, they had been separated for more than ten months, and she was starting proceedings for a divorce. The night of her death, she had booked herself an executive suite at The Savoy Hotel in London and drunk two bottles of Bollinger champagne. After slipping into the bathtub, she'd opened her brachial artery from wrist to elbow on both arms. It was determined that she would have lost consciousness in under a minute, and was dead within two.

A young, female police officer had delivered this news to Henry on the very doorstep over which the men from Graves, Inc. now brought Marjorie back to him. At the time, Henry hadn't quite understood what the officer was saying. The shock of it all pretty much numbed his entire being as she gave her condolences.

He could recall a single tear crawling down his right cheek, and just before he closed the door on her rhetoric, Henry thought he'd seen the police officer's eyes misting over too. This memory may well have been a flight of fancy however, because the days that followed were very dark and haphazard indeed.

The guilt was a cancer on his psyche – it ate away at him, drove him to the point of madness, and then left him living a waking dream, where fantasy and reality fused into one, and escape seemed impossible. Although at the time he had no need to escape. His desire was to be punished for the death of his wife, for he was – in his own mind – the conduit for her demise.

Had Henry not been so convinced that he needed to undergo such suffering, he may well have ended his own life, and in some ways, this may have been better as, somewhere along the road to attrition, Henry lost his way, and found himself on the path leading only to madness.

~

Henry thought he could try to make things up to Marjorie by spending time with her, to explain how he was sorry, how much he regretted what he'd done *to* her. He knew this was a strange enough thought even before contacting Graves, Inc., but as Halloween approached the idea had become more reasonable.

He'd found their number stuck to the announcement board in The Dirty Sow, a local pub most people avoided due to its unsavory reputation. There had been rumors it was the go-to place to arrange a hit; alleged and never proven, of course.

He'd found himself there after a particularly bad night on the whiskey, his brain so addled with alcohol he was impervious to the scowls and stares his entrance incurred from the regular, bawdy patrons. The business card on the wall merely said:

GRAVES, INC.
WE RETRIEVE AS YOU GRIEVE!
CALL NOW FOR PEACE OF MIND!

Henry had pulled the card from the board, rammed it into his pocket and left, staggering home where he'd collapsed, face down, into the flowerbed at the front of his house. The next time he thought about Graves, Inc. was when his idea to make his peace with Marjorie stopped seeming like insanity.

Within a few minutes of pulling the card from the pocket of his jacket, Henry had dialed the number. The rest had been so easy it had been almost criminal.

He didn't dwell too much on this latter fact.

~

"If you would be so kind as to wheel her into the dining room," Henry said to the men as they maneuvered Marjorie into the house on a rickety wheelchair. Marjorie was shrouded in a black body bag, a webbed belt about her middle keeping her in place as she was transported to the table. In her lap was another black bin-sack.

Henry pointed at the bag. "What's that?"

"Huh?" said Hardy.

Henry tutted. "The bag?"

"Dunno. Came with her."

"And what's inside it?" said Henry.

Laurel chuckled. "What do you *think* is inside it? Her *insides* are inside it."

Henry thought this over for a moment. "Well, I'm not sure we'll be in need of those."

"We don't do refunds," Laurel cautioned.

Henry nodded. "I understand. Please take them with you when you leave."

The men looked at each other and shrugged. "Suit yourself," said Laurel, dragging the bin-liner off Marjorie's lap and dropping it at his feet. There was a sloshing sound as the bag landed, and flattened out like a wide, fat Pontefract cake.

The men removed the dining chair and wheeled Marjorie up to the table. They stepped back and celebrated their handiwork by shaking hands with each other.

Hardy lifted the baseball cap and wiped sweat off his high forehead with his sleeve. "You might want to turn down the heating a bit. With the best will in the world, she's going to be ripe when you open the sack." He repositioned his cap. "You got any vapor-rub?"

Henry dug into his pocket and pulled out a green tub. "*Be prepared*, as the scouts say."

Both men nodded with approval. Laurel reached into his satchel and removed his clipboard. "Sign all three dockets, please."

Henry did as he was asked, Laurel checking the paperwork over before storing the clipboard away.

The men headed for the exit after Laurel hefted the bin sack containing Marjorie's innards. Before they disappeared through the front door, Hardy turned to Henry. "We were never here. Got that?"

With that, they were gone.

~

The roast was carved and placed at the center of the table, and the vegetables were heaped in oval porcelain dishes and large tureens. Henry served, the greasy heat of the decongestant trying its best to hold at bay the fierce stench coming off Marjorie. By the time Henry had plated up, he'd vomited twice in the Yucca plant pot, and once on his moccasins as he sat down to eat.

After vomiting onto his shoes, Henry dry-heaved several times, his mouth giving off multiple yawns, eyes watering, saliva swinging as a clear thread from his lips, and he forced himself upright to continue his conversation with Marjorie.

His voice was weak with effort. "Well, as I was saying, my love, this whole idea came from a conversation I had with my father. You remember how Harry had his funny little ways?"

Marjorie remained silent. The body bag was peeled down and bunched about her shoulders like the halter-neck of a cheap ball-gown, and dark juices dripped to the ground, creating oily puddles on the carpet. With great care Henry had tried to unwrap her, but no matter how gentle his movements, pieces still fell off, and by the time the potent stink of necrotic meat became so overpowering he almost passed out, he decided to cut his losses and leave his beloved Marjorie mostly covered.

Henry pressed on, his face whimsical as he recalled the antics of his father. "Dad would always insist Mum put on a good spread at Halloween. You remember what he used to say?" Henry dissolved into a fit of giggles, interspersed with coughs and bouts of dry heaving. "If you produce a feast, then those loved ones who are no longer with us can't help but visit on All Hallows' Eve. He really believed it. And I believe it too."

What was left of Marjorie's face remained impassive. One eye was shut, a sunken crater of moist flesh bisected by a zipper of tangled lashes. The other was open, but the socket was empty. Her mouth was a loose mix of bloated purple flesh and black goo.

Placing his hands on the table, Henry fought against his ongoing desire to vomit – his eyes were red from the stress of it, and his nostrils and upper lip were raw from the wads of vapor-rub he'd smeared over himself to counter the irrepressible stench.

"But I deserve this, Marjorie," he said. The tears – a mixture of grief and irritation from the decongestant – fell onto his dinner plate, merging with the congealed gravy covering his uneaten meal. "Yes, I deserve it all because I failed you. No, I didn't just fail you. I *killed* you."

Henry's voice melted, the sobs coming with great force. His hands went to his face, his fists ramming knuckles painfully into his eyes to stem the flow of hot tears. His chest pumped like a mangy cur after eating grass, and he gagged once more, dissolving into a coughing fit. He thumped the table in frustration, the plates and cutlery protesting with a unified clatter, shocking him back to the here and now.

Henry regained some composure, but any control he had was paltry, fragile.

He looked at his wife's ruined face. "Won't you come back to me?" he pleaded. He swept his hands above the table, the gesture grand, almost theatrical. "This feast is all for you. All the things you enjoyed when you were here, with me. I said I wanted something different, but I was wrong, I want you, only you. Please, Marjorie, I need you!"

Save for the occasional *plop* of something hitting the carpet, Marjorie remained silent, and in that moment, realisation began to dawn, awareness coming at him like a storm rolling in from the ocean, the futility and despair imbued in his idea of reconciliation now recognised for what it was: madness at the behest of guilt, pure and unbridled.

With the power of this newfound realisation came the reaction – the horror – of it all. As would the clear waters of a lake disturbed by a skimmed stone, the macabre scene before him wavered, his sense of perspective now off-kilter as the room appeared to spin – chairs, tables, gaudy wallpaper, liquified corpses of dead spouses, all fusing together in a dizzying maelstrom that had him pitching forward, his head striking the corner of the table as he went down.

As the darkness rushed in, turning his world to shadow, Henry thought he could hear soft, lilting laughter.

~

When awareness finally returned, Henry fought to comprehend what was going on about him. But even the strange tightness in his chest could not stem the incredible surge of excitement as he realised Marjorie was sitting opposite, no longer a leaking corpse but the woman who had left him months ago. Her dark hair was swept back into a tress, and the ball-gown she wore was bottle-green and adorned with intricate lace-work and small white gemstones.

She was sitting at the far end of the table, the candles between them creating an undulating sea of light. Marjorie delicately chewed on a morsel of food, and when she saw he was awake and looking at her, she placed the shimmering cutlery on the table and wiped her mouth with the corner of a napkin.

Marjorie smiled; eyes alive with sputtering flame. "I need to thank you, dear Henry. You were right about many things. Tonight is special: it *is* a time for loved ones to return. Just as you were right to reach out and make your peace with me. But more importantly, make peace with yourself."

Henry tried to return her smile, but his mouth wasn't quite ready to behave. His head throbbed, and he made to reach for his forehead to check out the damage from his fall.

Marjorie chuckled. "Yes. You are right about many things. And perhaps your greatest insight has significant poignancy in the afterlife. You see, when you *cross over*, things are very different

– right and wrong have no meaning. The things that define us in life no longer hold sway in what the people of this world call 'Death'."

It was as Henry tried to lift his right arm to rub at his forehead that he realised the limb was no longer there. In panic he looked down at himself, the horror snapping him back to consciousness as though doused in ice-cold water.

All his limbs were gone, taken from shoulder and hip joints, and the tightness about his chest was the belt from his trousers strapping his ruined torso to the dining-chair. He tried to scream, but found his mouth was now stuffed with the digits from his own hands. As he gagged, a thumb fell into his lap, where it wriggled like a fat grub in a pool of berry-red blood.

Through wide, terrified eyes he looked at the table, where his amputated limbs had been served up on platters, cooked and carved.

He watched Marjorie spear another piece of meat with her fork. She began to chew, and the squeak of Henry's flesh against her teeth made him weep.

She looked over to him, swallowed her food deliberately, her body shuddering with the apparent relish of it. "Don't cry, dear Henry. This is where you were right in more ways than you can imagine."

She tilted her head, grinning as grease ran down her chin. "There's always a need to try something a little different."

And Your Fear Shall Define You

"'And your fear shall define you'." Michael Holland shuffled in his seat, the waterproof material of his brown, mini-trench coat hissing like an irritated cat. "That's what she said."

Dr Sheridan sat opposite, one hand holding a fountain pen, the nib of which hovered over a sparse set of medical notes; the fingers of the other hand beat out a dull tattoo against his moleskin slacks. "That would be," he double-checked the file on his desk just to be sure, "the 'gypsy'?"

Michael's smile was wan, the doughy complexion of his cheeks stark against the heavy neon-blue visor shades and black *Top Gun* baseball cap. "Yes. I laughed at the time. They were just words, right? 'Sticks and stones' as the adage goes. Crazy talk from an arrogant woman."

Dr Sheridan swiveled in his chair, facing his patient. It was a Friday morning, and his thoughts were already turning to the driving range and dinner with his wife at Rossini's. Keeping his end-of-week diary clear was only ever usurped by an interesting case, and Michael Holland ticked the box, and then some. Local businessman and landowner of The Acorn Rural Initiative Ltd, Michael was a very private man, a bachelor of significant means, and him booking an appointment was as bizarre and unlikely as his choice of attire for the visit. The mini-trench coat was Gautier and conservative, but the pants ballooned with a bodacious lime green and yellow tiger-slash print, making him look like MC Hammer going through a manic episode. He added this observation to the assessment sheet as Michael continued, oblivious; his tone languid, as though they were friends chit-chatting over coffee.

"Curses. Hexes. I think I may have lost my mind along with everything else."

Sheridan answered softly, neutering his reverence at the opportunity to discuss such matters with his ubiquitous patient. "Have you considered the psychological implications of curses, Michael?"

Michael tilted his head to the left, a dog hearing something its owner could not. "What do you mean?"

"Well, in some ways you are quite right, they *are* just words. But, if people are so inclined, words can, and often *do*, hurt. If they are true or tap into the psyche of a vulnerable person, for example. In such instances they can get under the skin. The concept of curses and hexes and so forth work on this basis. Indeed, that is their design. Their very *nature*."

In response, Michael gave out a grunt and there was a series of tiny cracks and pops, the sounds not unlike those of an old man's knees when standing after a long afternoon sitting on his favourite futon. Dr Sheridan blinked a few times to clear the thought that his patient's arms and legs had grown a few inches since he'd last looked at them. From the street, INXS's *Devil Inside* found its way through the bow window. The tan loafer on Sheridan's right foot absently bounced in time with the beat.

"I never really saw *myself*," Michael continued. His demeanor was detached, his voice presenting as though keeping his own counsel. "I never realised exactly who I was until that day. Until she showed me. I could've made amends, but she was an abhorrence, that's how I saw *it* – her. It wasn't the first time I poured scorn on those I considered beneath me. I inherited more than an estate from my father, I also pocketed his lack of tolerance. So no surprise I should revert to type. I lay blame and mocked her whimsy. Her crime was far worse than mine, you see?"

"Crime?"

"Trespass."

Sheridan's eyebrows lifted. "She was camped on your land?"

"Yes. My father built our house – our home – on land he broke his back to buy. Putting our family out of poverty's clutches saw him into an early grave. He gave his life to that estate, to us. It is ours, damn it! Why should someone feel they can just put their wheels upon it, lay claim to it as though they have such right?"

The doctor made some more notes; the scratch of nib against vellum held its own rhythm. "I sense your frustration."

"I've been worse." Michael released a sigh, his shoulders sagging as though the very act was causing him to deflate like a cheap helium balloon from a second-rate vendor. "It seemed such a big deal back then. But time and circumstance do that to a problem, do they not? Demean it, make it trivial."

"Time does not quell the emotions as readily as we would like, Michael," Sheridan said, bouncing the lid of the pen barrel against his lower lip. "Our brain is an incredible piece of machinery. Its ability to compartmentalise that which ails us is remarkable. Nature's psychological sticking plaster, if you will. But it is exactly that, a sticking plaster on a deep wound. Soon something bad is bound to leak out. And I say that is where we are at this moment."

The blue visor shimmered as Michael scanned the diplomas and degrees on the wall behind Sheridan, a lifetime of great achievement condensed to a set of matching gold and brown frames.

"Look at you. On display for all to see. You know your place in this world, Doctor. And the world knows you. Grounded, that is what I see in this office. A man of science who is destined to listen to my woes and I fear will see only madness."

"Is it madness to examine who we are of ourselves? No matter how such a thing came to pass?"

"Perhaps. Perhaps not."

As though inclined to his words, Michael nodded, the movement slight and without vigour, yet his visor seemed to push forwards, as though something was pressing against the frames. His baseball cap shivered, giving the impression there was some creature eager to get out from under it.

"I never meant to do what I did. The fire, I mean. It was an accident."

Sheridan perked a little. "You've not mentioned a fire."

"Have I not?"

"No. Do you wish to talk about it now?"

"She'd lit a fire pit. I can see her now hunched over it, a rabbit carcass on a spit, rotating it with her fingers." He paused, suddenly and with a thoughtful air. "Did I say her fingers reminded me of twigs, dried twigs that I used to find at the base of oak trees in autumn as a boy on the estate?"

"You did not."

"Well, that's exactly what they looked like, and when I came across her, looking as though our land belonged to her, that she had a right to be there, I had such a rage in my belly. And she was singing, a gentle refrain I came to identify with some research in the town library. *The Bitter Willow* was its name, oddly beautiful now I think about it. And I think about it often. Dream of it, even. I think it haunts me, a reminder of her, should I ever forget. Like I ever could. She has a power, and it holds such sway. Yet all I could see back then was someone holding my father – and all he'd worked for – in contempt."

"And you kicked at the fire pit?" Such was the intrigue, Sheridan's question came a little too eager, making him feel like a town gossip at Saturday Market.

"Not straight away. First of all, I asked her what the hell she thought she was doing on private property."

"And what was her response?"

"Her response? Why she just smiled as if I had merely asked her the time."

"And *then* you kicked the fire pit?"

"You are too keen for me to do so, Dr Sheridan. There *was* kicking, but not at that point. I was too stunned by that harridan's gall. Taken aback was an understatement for sure. For a few seconds I was struck dumb. And in those moments the woman spoke, and her words merely added fuel to the fire in my gut."

"And what *were* her words, Michael?"

"She told me that neither earth, sea, wind or air had a master. That the elements were free of the world of men and were beholden only to themselves."

Sheridan leaned forwards, expectant. "And then?"

Michael chuckled. "And, yes, *then* I kicked the fire pit. But it was in temper, a wanton act, a fierce sense of duty to my father's honour. But the grease from the coney, the well-established flames, they sprayed so effectively, so thoroughly, and the woman's cart was mere wood and paint. The whole thing went up like straw in the height of summer. And it was spectacular, to say the least; mesmerising, even. I had trouble taking my eyes off of it, that beautiful, terrible sight. But it was the agonised screams of the woman that brought me out of my stupor."

"Was she hurt?"

"Not physically, no. But she yelled about all her worldly goods now gone forever, heirlooms and belongings of her family long past. That was when she turned to me and said those fearful words. That was when my fate was in her hands, and she crushed my future to oblivion."

"What happened to her afterwards?"

"That was the strangest thing. Well, I say 'strangest' but what I mean is it was the strangest thing *back then*. Because no sooner had she said those words, I responded by laughing so hard that I inhaled woodsmoke and began coughing. Once the fit ended, she was gone."

"Gone?"

"Not a sign. As though she'd never been there at all."

"But she *had* been there?"

"Yes, of course. The caravan was still there, burning. But the harridan was nowhere to be seen."

"Seems strange that she didn't stay. To hold you to account for your actions."

"She'd already done her worst. Her words truly were a weapon. I am damned. I realised this soon after her disappearance."

"How so?"

"I'm *changing*, Dr Sheridan. I am *becoming* something else."

"So you say, Michael. And I am here to assess in what ways. Yet since your arrival, you seem reticent to allow me to perform any sort of physical examination. It is as though you are in conflict with assumption and reality."

"I *am* changing. There is no doubt in my mind."

"And can you give me a hint as to what makes you think this way?"

"Apart from the hexes of an aggrieved witch?"

"What has *changed*?" Sheridan gently pressed.

"Appetites."

"Diet or desire?"

"Both."

"Care to explain?"

"Three days ago, I ate a rat."

The doctor sat back in his chair. "A rat, you say?"

"Yes. A cellar rat. It was quite delicious." Michael smiled.

"I see. And how did you prepare the rodent for eating?" The doctor's pen was once more poised over paper.

"I ate it as I'd found it. It did wriggle somewhat, but I crushed it in my hands first. Just to take the fight out of it."

Sheridan's pallor seemed to blanch. "Oh. And how did engaging in such an act make you feel?"

"Oddly satisfied."

"And have you eaten any other rats since?"

"Several. But the most recent failed to sate my hunger. As I say, my appetites seem wanton."

"And your desires?"

"I feel nothing."

"Nothing?" Sheridan pressed.

"I am emotionally barren, doctor. An empty vessel without an ounce of care, be it fair or foul."

"Do you attribute this to the woman's words also?"

"Can there be any other reason? Ask anyone in this town of me and my nature, and they would have told of a passionate man, a man of principle, a patriot. A man prepared to speak his mind and joust with those spineless protestors who dither in a world made impotent by fear of being labelled *immoral*."

"And what would they say of you now?"

"I truly do not care. And there lies the problem. Apathy is now my companion. Apathy and a yearning the like of which I cannot describe. A *restlessness* without aim, an itch without any means to scratch it calm. The man I was is gone. Now, I'm not sure if..."

The pause was pronounced, as if Michael was realising something for the very first time.

"What is it?" There was a tiny jitter in the doctor's voice. Of concern. Of apprehension.

"I'm not sure if I'm *still a man at all.*"

Sheridan let out a sigh. "Come, come. Let's not be too hasty. Let me do an exam. Remove your coat and we can put your mind at ease."

"There's no need, doctor. I must accept my lot. I've outgrown my own convention. I am a thing, an entity that should not exist. Not here, not in this time. Yet I am born, my mother a harridan from a burning cart, and I wear her curse like a vile keepsake."

"Not exist, you say? You are here, flesh and blood and corporeal to say the least."

"Flesh and blood *is* now the medium by which I shall reform. Don't you see that, doctor?"

Michael's body quivered, for the briefest of moments, the material of his coat and harem pants becoming an oscillating landscape before being pulled taut as the body beneath seemed to suddenly expand.

"Behold!"

There was a series of tearing sounds as the fibres gave out under the strain, and the clothing was slowly shed, the way a snake discards its outmoded skin. Sheridan should have been horrified but Michael's previous observations had been accurate, the good doctor was a man of science, and what was happening before his eyes was a thing of terrible, if inexplicable, wonder. Something to be observed and understood, and he was here to bear witness to the scientific marvel unfolding before him.

"Fascinating."

"You need to leave."

Michael's voice was now a discordant baritone, each ululation made Sheridan's sternum shudder. The glass rattled against the window frames, the resulting hum was eerily beautiful and ambiguous.

With a pistol-shot crack, the armrests on Michael's chair gave out against his ever-expanding hips. One armrest flopped, the other detached and clattered upon the beige linoleum floor tiles. "Leave while you still can. I can only see the world as she intended, a place to fear, a place to sate my needs."

He stood, the movement making him groan, his height now implausibly tall, so tall in fact that his crown scraped the ceiling, dislodging the baseball cap which fell away from his bloated, bald scalp, skittering off of his broad, pale shoulder, and slapping at his feet. The visor followed seconds later, and it was when Sheridan looked upon Michael's completely exposed face for the very first time that the physician finally gave out a whimper of abject terror.

The mouth was by now rimmed with fat, navy-coloured lips, which glistened wetly under the florescent lights. Beyond the lips were a zipper of rectangular teeth, uneven and yellow. But it was the sheen of moisture tickling down Michael's malformed features, circumventing the broad, flat nose, lapped away from his sloppy mouth by a yellowed tongue, that stunned Sheridan. It was a cataract of tears from a single, bloodshot eye at the centre of the forehead, mesmerising in its presence, the blackness of the iris indistinguishable from that of the pupil, and peering out from beneath cowled lids of heavy, puckered flesh.

"Incredible," Sheridan breathed, despite his fear. "Absolutely incredible."

"One eye to reflect my assumed view of the world. My endless myopic tears: to purge the vision of distain I bore upon others. The witch is a woman of humour, I shall give acknowledgement to this talent. Just as I much acknowledge what I have become, a beast determined by myth, and driven by the most basic of needs."

There was no sudden effort, no animalistic pouncing, just a sedate *reaching* for the doctor, and an opening of thick fingers and the meat of a great palm. The hand grabbed at the physician, clutching him about the upper bicep of his right arm. The twist of a wrist later came with staccato clicks and a loud squelch as the limb was torn free, flesh and fabric became one between Michael's tombstone teeth.

"You taste so *learned*, Dr Sheridan. Just as I thought you might." He chewed hungrily, the tears still falling from that hooded eye, his vision spangled, the meat turning the tang of his mouth metallic. The doctor crumpled, the blood venting from his tattered shoulder, and with a sickening creak, his head hit the side of the desk on his way to the floor. The eyes that looked at Michael's burgeoning, twisted toes saw nothing at all.

Michael now wept at Sheridan's vacant stare. "I gave you chance, damn you! More than that given to me. But now I must give in to who I am. I cannot stop it. I'm sorry. I'm sorry!"

Feral and merciless, the great beast fell upon the doctor's inert body. Those same mighty hands brutalised the abdomen, opening it like a refuse sack, and rummaging within the cavity. Soft and delicate innards were scooped into an eager maw and guzzled like a vile feast exalting only the death of reason.

When the deed was done, Michael sank to his knees, head bowed, his bare, barrelled chest heaving. A viscous pink rivulet – blood and tears and sinewed meat – fell to pool about him, his body convulsing with awful sobs.

"You are dead, but I am forever damned."

Two small taps on the air broke into his lament. The office door opened seconds later and the face of the receptionist, sallow and shocked beneath a black bob, gawped in disbelief through the crack between jamb and doorframe. Seconds later, the scream cut through and Michael, nude and bloodied, was on his feet and slamming his bulk into the door, taking it through the frame and smashing it – and the unfortunate receptionist behind it – into the opposing wall of the corridor outside. There was the splintering of wood, the crack of breaking bones and a jet of crimson slashing across the magnolia paintwork. A picture was knocked askew, a huge crack in the plaster dislodging it so that the image of geese climbing lazily into the sky now appeared as though the gaggle were intent on finding freedom via a suicide run back to earth.

Michael staggered up the corridor, the door and the shattered receptionist now forgotten. Instead, his mind was focused on getting free of the building. There was a compulsion within him, especially now that he had sated his need to feed, and that compulsion demanded he leave the town and return to the vast acreage of the family estate, back to where his roots lay. He craved the woodlands and the forests he knew to be beyond brick and metal and glass, and the caves where he could hide. Part of him cried out for what he once was, a man of means who was a slave to his own prejudice. And there was a knowing, although it was fading fast, that he had indeed become the thing that he feared above all else. He was a pariah, the beggar in the doorway, the benefit-languishing parasite feeding from the state, the person without value... or without the values Michael had held in esteem before *Becoming*. This was the true curse, this was his penance for prejudice, and he would be alone and feared and despised forever.

He stormed out of the surgery, rendering wood and glass, and those he came across in the street, looking upon his gore-streaked nakedness, were afraid and repulsed in equal measure. They shied away, and he ran, scared and desperate to be free of the sudden, crushing oppression of brick and mortar. He ploughed through hedgerows, knocked aside turnstile and gate, until all that lay before him was a patchwork landscape of trees and fields.

His cavernous nostrils took in the air, and it brought with it the sweet scent of liberty. He thudded towards his haven, and although he briefly revelled in his freedom, there was no escaping the nuance born to him from the witch's curse, an element that gnawed at him the way he had gnawed at the doctor's bones. An element to forever remind him of his fate.

The soft lilting chorus of an old gypsy song; *The Bitter Willow* now an eternal melody of regret. Head bowed, his tears falling, the cyclops entered the estate, where the forest, like the gypsy's refrain, lay waiting to consume him.

Also by Dave Jeffery:

Novels
Frostbite (Severed Press, 2017)
A Quiet Apocalypse (Demain Publishing, 2019)
Labyrinth (Severed Press, 2020)
Cathedral (Demain Publishing, 2021)
The Samaritan (Demain Publishing, 2021)
Tribunal (Demain Publishing, 2022)
The Devil Device (Crossroad Press, 2023)

Visit Dave Jeffery at his website:
www.davejefferyauthor.com

Now available and forthcoming from Black Shuck Shadows:

Now available and forthcoming from Black Shuck Shadows:

Now available and forthcoming from Black Shuck Shadows:

Now available and forthcoming from
Black Shuck Shadows:

Shadows 37 – Dirt Upon My Skin

by Steve Toase

blackshuckbooks.co.uk/shadows

Milton Keynes UK
Ingram Content Group UK Ltd.
UKHW040902180724
445738UK00004B/30